LIVE
FROM BRENTWOOD HIGH

Price of Silence

LIVE
FROM BRENTWOOD HIGH

Price of Silence

JUDY BAER

BETHANY HOUSE PUBLISHERS
MINNEAPOLIS, MINNESOTA 55438

Price of Silence
Judy Baer

Cover illustration by Joe Nordstrom

Library of Congress Catalog Card Number 93–94538

ISBN 1–55661–387–3

Published by Bethany House Publishers
A Ministry of Bethany Fellowship, Inc.
11300 Hampshire Avenue South
Minneapolis, Minnesota 55438

Printed in the United States of America

To Connie B.—who loves to laugh.

JUDY BAER received a B.A. in English and Education from Concordia College in Moorhead, Minnesota. She has had over thirty novels published and is a member of the National Romance Writers of America, the Society of Children's Book Writers, and the National Federation of Press Women.

Two of her novels, *Adrienne* and *Paige*, have been prizewinning bestsellers in the Bethany House SPRINGFLOWER SERIES (for girls 12–15). Both books have been awarded first place for juvenile fiction in the National Federation of Press Women's communications contest.

LIVE

FROM BRENTWOOD HIGH

CHAPTER 1

LIVE

FROM DRENTWOOD HIGH

Molly Ashton blew into the *Live! From Brentwood High* media room like a hurricane, knocking books off desks and a sheaf of papers from a counter. The workroom and adjacent television studio—aptly nicknamed "Chaos Central"—had become a major hub of activity for Molly and the other students working on news stories and features for the student-run television station at Brentwood High.

Isador Mooney, Andrew Tremaine, and Jake Sanders were in the audio room tinkering with the control board through which sound was patched, mixed, amplified, and distributed. The booth had visual contact with the studio through a glass wall.

Izzy was waving his hands and yelling—at least it appeared he was yelling, since no noise could escape the room except through an intercom. His face was red to the stubbly roots of his buzz-cut hair and his fair skin blotchy with frustration.

"What's going on in there?" Molly asked.

"Creative differences." Darby Ellison grimaced. "Izzy thinks he knows everything and Jake and Andrew think he knows nothing."

Darby's shoulder-length hair was a tumble of dark

curls. She tugged on a stray lock that had fallen into her eyes. "I'm glad they're disagreeing where they can't be heard. It's loud enough out here already."

"That's an understatement," Molly observed sourly. Kate Akima and Julie Osborn were arguing over a program log to be posted in the studio. Sarah Riley, Josh Willis, and Shane Donahue were watching an old *Three Stooges* video on one side of the room while their instructor, Rosie Wright, and her assistant, Gary Richmond, were reviewing the video of last week's program on the other.

"Would everyone please just *shut up!*"

Immediately Julie and Kate quit talking. Josh reached for the volume control on the television. Even Ms. Wright punched the button on her remote, and the picture she and Gary were watching faded away.

"Wake up on the wrong side of the bed today, Ashton?" Julie inquired with mock sweetness. "Or just decide to let us see your real personality for a change?"

"Lay off, Julie. I might not be a prize today, but I don't see any blue ribbon on you either."

Surprise washed across Julie's features. Molly was not usually into quick, sarcastic retorts.

"Relax." Darby brushed a hand across Molly's arm and felt the tension radiating from her body. "Julie's just being Julie."

"Well, she should stop it and turn into something human for a while." Molly's behavior was so unnatural that everyone in the room stared at her as she shook Darby's hand away. "And I wish everybody would leave me alone!"

"What's *wrong*, Molly?" Darby persisted gently. "I've never seen you like this before."

Molly's golden curls quivered as she clamped her lips tightly together and stormed across the room. She dropped her book bag onto a desk and pulled out a ring-binder notebook. "Excuse me if I don't feel like talking. I've got a lot of work to do."

"Grouch!" Julie muttered under her breath and turned back to Kate. "Ignore her."

Gary leaned backward in his chair and cupped his hands behind his head; his gray-green eyes narrowed in thought. He crossed one jean-clad leg over the other and stared at the tense young woman across from him. His chiseled jaw tightened as he tugged thoughtfully on the earring in his left earlobe.

Gary had spent a hard, exciting life as a photojournalist and field producer for national television news teams before burning out on the starvation and desperation in Somalia and the heartbreak of the civil war in Bosnia. He'd come to Brentwood at the request of Ms. Wright to work with her on the student-run cable channel. Gary was tough and savvy—and surprisingly perceptive.

He is a good example of the old adage "Looks are deceiving," Darby mused. After all, Julie Osborn and Andrew Tremaine looked just fine—no shaggy ponytails or disheveled clothing—and they were both major pains in the neck!

"Will everyone gather over here please?" Ms. Wright tapped her pen against a water glass on the desk. "We have to begin considering topics for upcoming features. Because we're working under such tight deadlines, you may be working on more than one story and with more than one team at a time. Any ideas?"

Sarah Riley maneuvered her wheelchair nearer to

Ms. Wright's desk. "We're never going to find a story as good as the last one. That had drama, excitement, humor..."

"And the birth of a baby!"

"I agree. It was a very exciting feature on teenage emergency medical technicians, but certainly not the *only* story with those qualities. Besides, you can't look backward in television. There's no time. It's a very hungry medium. We always have to be thinking about the *next* story, not the last one."

"How about something on the destruction of the natural habitat of animals in our region?" Izzy suggested. He was an animal fanatic who often took in stray dogs and cats—and once a displaced ferret.

"If I'm going to do a story on wildlife," Andrew sneered, "it's going to be about the weekend parties in Brentwood."

"My dad's putting me on a budget," Kate offered. "How about a story on managing your finances?"

"Borr-ring," Shane growled.

"Then *you* think of something! My mind is blank."

"Obviously."

"That's enough!" Ms. Wright cut off the brewing confrontation.

"This is *hard*," Julie complained. "Can't you give us some ideas?"

"You knew you'd be responsible for picking out story topics. Hasn't anyone been thinking?"

"A thousand ways to cook macaroni and cheese!" Izzy blurted. "Why, I must have four hundred recipes of my own!"

"Or fashion-consciousness for the color-blind," Kate retorted. "Izzy knows all about that too."

Ms. Wright shook her head in exasperation. "We need something hard-hitting, topical—*meaningful*. Sorry, Izzy, it's not that I don't think your life is meaningful, but cooking mac and cheese and wearing clothes that clash isn't exactly what I had in mind."

Molly, who had been grimly doodling on her notebook looked up. "I wish everyone would quit being so childish. Why don't you give her some *real* suggestions?"

"If you're so smart, why don't *you*?" Julie retorted.

Two words exploded from Molly. "Sexual harassment!"

The room filled with surprised silence.

"What did you say?" Ms. Wright asked.

"Sexual harassment," Molly repeated softly. "In school and on the job."

"That's no better!" Julie began. "If that's your great idea . . ."

"Wait." Ms. Wright held up a hand. "It's a *good* idea—relevant, timely, emotional. I like it. What do the rest of you think?"

Shane shrugged. "It's okay with me."

"Me too."

"I guess so," Julie relented. "Besides, I hate macaroni and cheese."

"Fine," Ms. Wright concluded briskly. "Molly, since you suggested the idea, I'd like you to be on this team. Andrew, your father owns a business. That might be helpful when you're doing research. Anyone else like to volunteer?"

Josh raised his hand. "I would."

"Me too," Darby volunteered. "I think it sounds like a great topic."

"Fine. I'd like to have one more on this team. This may involve a lot of interviews. Who's completed their other assignments and is free to work on this?"

Reluctantly Kate raised her hand. Everyone knew she preferred to work with her best friend, Julie, but Ms. Wright's pointed stare forced her hand into the air.

"Wonderful. I'll expect a comprehensive, thought-provoking piece on sexual harassment. Now, as for the rest of you . . ."

Ms. Wright briskly made assignments for pieces for the radio show and newspaper articles also done by the *Live!* group before opening the television production textbook on her desk. "Today we're going to talk more about camera movements. As you already know, 'left' and 'right' refer to the camera's point of view. . . ."

Darby, Molly, Josh, and the other team members held back as the rest of the students flooded into the hallway after class.

"What do you think of the new assignment?" Kate asked. "Can we do it?"

"We *have* to do it. We don't have any choice."

"I think it will be interesting," Josh said. "I've experienced harassment for being black, but I'd never thought much about women being harassed for being female."

"I think," Andrew muttered, "that this topic is highly overrated. Harassment is just a myth if you ask me."

"So no one asked you!" Molly stared at the floor, her eyes fixed and glassy.

"Molly, are you all right?"

"Great. Just great."

But if things were so great, then why did Molly look as though she were waiting to have a tooth pulled?

———

"I thought you'd already left." The unexpected sound caused Darby to jump and hit her head on the inside edge of her locker.

"Owww!" She rubbed at her injury. "Kate, you startled me!"

"So I see. Why didn't you go with Josh and Molly?"

"Have you seen the inside of my locker? It looks like I'm raising gerbils in there. I thought I'd clean it out before the health inspector closes it down." Darby looked around for Julie. "Are you alone?"

"Julie couldn't wait. Doctor appointment or something." Kate tapped her foot against the tile floor. "I could give you a ride home if you want."

"S-sure." The unexpected invitation caught Darby off guard. Kate and Julie were notorious for excluding other girls from their twosome. "Do you mind if I stop in the rest room? I think I need to comb my hair."

"The school emptied out early tonight," Kate commented. "Of course, I don't blame anyone for not hanging around. Hurry up, will you?"

Darby led the way into the rest room. She might have run a comb through her hair and left if she had not heard two girls talking at the far end of the room.

"My brother told me about it. Can you believe it?"

"In the guys' locker room? Are you sure?"

"Positive. My brother said that no teachers ever use that bathroom, and the janitors clean in there with the doors open. That's why they haven't seen the writing."

Kate's dark eyebrow arched upward, and she put a finger to her lips, signaling Darby to be silent.

"What does it say?"

"Names, mostly. And phone numbers. According to my brother, some of the names had . . . commentary . . . with them."

"What does that mean?"

"You know, stuff like 'Call Melanie for a great time' or 'Geri puts out'. . . that kind of stuff."

"Gross! Your brother didn't see my name there, did he?"

As the two girls came around the corner, Kate, who'd been holding the bathroom door open, allowed it to fall shut, making it appear that she and Darby had just entered.

Kate smiled sweetly at the two girls. "Hi, did I hear you say something about Melanie and Geri? I have a cousin named Melanie. She doesn't go to school here, of course, but . . ."

The two girls looked uncomfortable and indecisive. Finally one of them spoke. "If your cousin doesn't go to school here, then this has nothing to do with her. We were just talking about some stuff my brother saw in the boys' locker room."

"Stuff?"

"Graffiti. Crude junk. Apparently the guys think it's funny to scratch obscene things about girls on the doors inside the stalls."

Darby and Kate both tensed. Kate pressed her hand against Darby's arm to silence her. "What do the girls whose names are on the walls have to say about this?"

"I don't know. I *do* know that I don't want *my* name there. What a crummy feeling that would be!"

With that, the two girls walked out of the room, leaving Kate and Darby to stare at each other in dismay.

"I guess Molly was right on target," Kate said quietly. "That sounds like sexual harassment to me—right here at Brentwood High."

"Of all the dumbest, ickiest, most juvenile things I've ever heard . . ." Darby fumed as she and Kate left the rest room. "I can't believe guys would do something so childish." She didn't look up until she ran full tilt into Izzy.

"You'd better start looking where you're going," he commented lazily as he held Darby by the upper arms. "Otherwise you're going to hurt yourself—or me."

"Sorry, Izzy. I guess I was blind with rage."

"Sounds serious," Jake said from behind Izzy. "What's going on?"

"Do you know what's been happening in the boys' locker room?"

"Yeah, but I'd rather not talk about it."

Darby gave Izzy a black look. "Don't be funny. Do you know about the writing on the walls?"

Izzy and Jake exchanged a cautious glance. "What do you mean?"

"Spill it, guys. Tell us what they're writing in there."

"Not everyone is doing it," Jake said. "But a few guys have got this competition going to see who can write the rudest, crudest stuff. It's gotten out of hand, but I thought the guys were keeping it to themselves."

"Are there a lot of girls' names written in there?"

Jake looked down at his shoes. Izzy stuffed his hands into his pockets, and a flush ran up his neck.

"Aren't you going to answer my question?"

"Just a couple names," Izzy mumbled. "Gerilyn McDonald mostly."

"*That* Geri? The Geri who is so quiet I've never even heard her voice?"

"That's the one."

"But *why*?"

"Somebody must have thought it was funny—especially because Gerilyn is so shy. Now her name has become part of the joke."

"Why haven't you done something about this?" Darby demanded. "Can't you *stop* them?"

"How? We don't even know who's doing it. Sometimes I erase the stuff that's written in pencil, but lately there have been words etched into the paint."

"I can't believe you guys didn't tell us about this!" Kate fumed.

"Why? What could you do about it?"

"Izzy, you big dope, don't you get it? This is *exactly* what we're covering for our story. If this isn't sexual harassment, I don't know what is!"

Izzy stared, blinking at Kate for a moment before a dawning look crossed his features. "Oh, yeah, I guess it is." He looked shamefaced. "I didn't think much about it. Stuff like that happens all the time in locker rooms."

"That's exactly our point! Can you imagine how angry and humiliated Gerilyn would feel if she knew what was being said about her?"

"I think she *does* know," Jake said regretfully. "I saw Gerilyn leaving school this afternoon just before last hour. She was crying."

How could anyone do something so hateful?

"Wait up!" Darby hurried after Josh and Molly as they walked down the hallway toward the studio.

When Josh saw Darby, a smile split his face. "We were afraid you wouldn't be coming. Sarah said you had a test to make up this afternoon."

"I took it during noon hour. I didn't want to miss our meeting." Darby moved into step beside them. Josh towered over the girls, his slenderness accentuating his height.

"Good. We need you." Josh always knew what to say to make someone feel special, wanted. His dark eyes twinkled warmly as his gaze traveled from Darby to Molly and back again. "Besides, I'm going to look really good when I walk in with all the brainpower in the group beside me."

"Yeah, right," Molly groused. "I've got the 'brainpower' of a flea."

"I hear fleas are very intelligent insects."

Even Molly had to laugh. She curled her hand into a fist and punched Josh in the arm. "I was having a good time being crabby. Quit cheering me up."

"Sorry. I didn't realize you were enjoying it. Around my house, no one is *allowed* to be crabby."

"You've got rules?"

"Sort of. My mother says that if I'm grumpy, then she'd better give me something to be grumpy about. I usually end up cleaning the litter box, washing windows, or hauling out trash. It doesn't pay to be in a bad mood!"

"Now *that's* depressing!"

"Tell us about your family, Josh," Darby encouraged in an attempt to distract Molly from whatever was eating at her. "You don't have any brothers or sisters going to Brentwood High, do you?"

"No. I have a little brother at Harbor Elementary and an older sister who is married. My mom teaches third grade at Harbor, and my dad is principal at the middle school."

"Surrounded by teachers day and night—bummer!"

Josh grinned at Molly. "My parents complain too. They say they're surrounded by *kids* day and night."

"Your parents sound just like mine," Molly said grimly. "They've got an answer for everything . . . they think. If they only knew. . . ."

Darby shrugged, her hands splayed in front of her, indicating to Josh that she had no idea what had put Molly into such a foul mood. Her fits of temper had become a regular occurrence the past few days. Everyone in the studio had been on the receiving end of one of Molly's sarcastic remarks.

"Looks like the others are already here." Josh deftly changed the subject. He tipped his head toward the audio room, where they were huddled over the control board. "I wonder if they know what they're doing."

At that moment Rosie Wright popped up from behind a turntable. She was dressed in a flowing skirt and a tie-dyed man's shirt knotted at her waist. Huge earrings, which vaguely resembled the lids from soup cans, dangled from her ears. "Looks like Ms. Wright is giving them some pointers."

"Where *does* she buy her clothes?" Molly asked, her bad mood unabated. "A secondhand shop?"

"I like her clothes. She looks relaxed, comfortable . . ."

"And exotic?" Josh concluded.

"She looks like she's trapped in the sixties to me."

"I heard that." Ms. Wright's voice came booming into the room over the PA. Molly had forgotten about the public address system.

"And thank you, Molly," she said as Molly's face turned the color of the red crepe paper streamers straggling off a half-finished bulletin board. "I was once advised to find a clothing style that suited me and to stick with it. Apparently I've succeeded."

"Sorry, Ms. Wright. I've been putting my foot in my mouth all day. Pretty soon I'll have a path worn on my tongue."

"Forgiven." Ms. Wright smiled and switched off the speaker.

"I'm glad she's so cool," Molly breathed. "What a dumb thing to say. What's wrong with my head these days?"

"Good question," Josh said bluntly. He studied Molly's face with warm, gentle eyes.

"Oh, Josh . . ." For a second it appeared that Molly might actually tell them what was going on with her. "I can't talk about it. Just skip it." The moment passed.

"Are you ready and eager to work?" Ms. Wright inquired as she whirled out of the sound booth with Andrew and Kate in her wake. "I hope so. After the success of the emergency medical technician story, I'm really excited to get going on this. I've been impressed with everyone's work. You've put out a television show, a radio program, and begun to lay out a newspaper article that all show a great deal of creativity and care. You should be proud."

Rosie Wright didn't give compliments easily or insincerely. Darby and Josh shared a satisfied grin.

"Since everyone is doing so well, I'm going to begin giving each of you more than one project to work on at a time. I want to get a few more features in the can . . ."

"In the can?"

"Taped. Shot. Done. *Finis*. A bumper. A cushion. Extra tapes so that if we don't finish a story on time, we will have something else to show in its place. We can always go live, of course, considering that the name of our show *is* "Live! From Brentwood High." But you really need a little experience and practice before we try that. Now, about the sexual harassment story . . ."

The school's public address system flickered to life with a crackle. "Ms. Wright? Long-distance phone call in the office."

"Be right there." She moved toward the door but paused at the threshold. "You can start planning your strategy. Take notes. When I get back, we can go over them together." In a flurry of cotton gauze and exotic perfume, she was gone.

"Where do we start?" Josh opened his notebook and drew a pencil out of his pocket.

"What did you do first on the EMT story, Darby?" Kate's dark, almond-shaped eyes glittered with admiration. "Whatever you did turned out all right."

Darby rubbed her hand through her curls. "We just fell into it, I guess. We'd better not plan on such good luck every time. Izzy, Jake, and I started doing interviews while Molly, Sarah, and Andrew did research at the library."

"Then let's do the same thing." Kate was an honor student at Brentwood and not about to let an *A* grade slip past her in this class. "Andrew and I will start in the library while—"

"Wait a minute! Speak for yourself," Andrew protested.

"You'd rather work on interviews? Okay, if that's what you want . . ."

"I don't 'want' to do either," Andrew said bluntly. "I don't even see what you're getting so excited about. I think we've got a 'non-topic' here."

"What's that supposed to mean?" Kate balled her fists and put her hands on her hips.

"Just what I said. How can I report on a subject that I don't even believe exists?"

Darby, Kate, and Josh stared at Andrew, mouths gaping.

"Don't look at me like that! You know what I mean. Sexual harassment is something women made up just to get back at men they don't like."

Darby pounded at the side of her head with her hand. "I don't believe I'm hearing this!"

"You've gone too far this time, Andrew," Kate fumed. "Of all the macho, egotistical, *stupid* statements I've ever heard . . ."

"Wait a minute before you get a rope and try to lynch me." Even Andrew seemed startled by the intensity of the girls' response. "Aren't you going to let me explain?"

"It had better be good."

"Have either of you ever been sexually harassed?" Andrew asked.

Kate and Darby looked at each other. "Not really, but that doesn't mean it doesn't exist."

"Has anyone you *know* been harassed?"

"I guess I never really thought about it but—"

"That's my point! You two are getting all worked up over something that isn't even real. Neither of you would let a guy get by with anything 'funny,' would you? I mean, look at how you jumped down my neck just now! We're talking the nineties here! Modern women! I don't buy the idea that sexual harassment exists anymore. Maybe it did once, but—"

"Hold on a minute, Andrew." Josh's voice was soft but firm. "Just because you haven't seen it doesn't mean that it doesn't exist. That's a pretty narrow view."

"What do you know about it?"

"I understand harassment," Josh said, his gentle eyes growing dark. "I've seen a lot of it in my life. Maybe it hasn't been sexual harassment, but I don't see much difference between being harassed because God made you a woman or because He made you black."

"Aw, I don't want to get into a race thing right now. I don't care if you're green, Josh!"

"Maybe *you* don't, but a lot of people do care. They care if I eat in 'their' restaurants, go to 'their' movies, or get in 'their' way. I've seen it and felt it, firsthand."

"It can't be all that bad," Andrew huffed. "Just stay away from people like that!"

"I could, if they all wore signs saying 'I'm prejudiced,' but they don't. There are people who don't respect women either. There are those who think that women, minorities, the disadvantaged, and the handicapped are fair game for insults, put-downs, and second-class treatment."

"Are you crawling up on a soapbox to give us this lecture, Josh? If you are, you might as well crawl right down again because I don't believe it. *You people*," and he stared inclusively at Darby, Kate, and Josh, "are making a big deal out of nothing."

A major fight might have erupted at that moment, if not for Molly's quiet sobbing in the corner.

They all heard the muffled cries at once. Darby and Kate hurried to the table where Molly sat. Josh and Andrew followed.

"What is it, Molly?" Kate demanded. "What's going on?"

"Let me talk to her." Darby knelt down by Molly's chair. "What's wrong?" she whispered gently. "What did we say that upset you?"

"How do you know it's our fault?" Andrew protested. Josh and Kate glared him into silence.

"Molly?" Josh dropped to one knee beside Darby. "Whatever it is, if we upset you, let us know. We can't fix something if we don't know what we've done wrong."

"It's . . . not . . . you," Molly hiccuped. She looked up at Josh with swollen, tear-filled eyes. "It's what you were talking about."

"My color?"

"N-no."

"Andrew's big mouth?" Kate muttered.

"H-he's *wrong*." Molly curled her arms across her chest and rocked back and forth as if to hold out the pain that was engulfing her.

"You bet he is. Jerk." Kate was unforgiving. She glared at Andrew, who glared back.

"Sexual ... harassment ..." Molly choked out the words as though they burned her throat. "It's not made up. It's real. It's happened to me. And I hate it. I *hate* it!"

CHAPTER 3

LIVE

FROM BRENTWOOD HIGH

Andrew's jaw went slack. A horrified expression rushed over his features. Darby and Kate were struck motionless for a moment, trying to comprehend Molly's statement. Only Josh seemed to realize what Molly had said. Gently, he took her hand and held it in his own. "It's going to be okay, Molly. It will. We'll help you."

Darby put an arm around Molly's shoulders while Kate fluttered her hands helplessly.

"I didn't want to tell you. I didn't want to tell anyone, but it just slipped out. I should never, *never*, have suggested the topic to Ms. Wright. It's just that I can't forget . . ." Her voice trailed away.

"I think we'd better talk this out." Darby pulled up a chair and sat down across from Molly. Josh, Kate, and finally Andrew followed her lead.

"I don't want to talk. There's nothing you can do. What's the point?"

"The point is, that one of the neatest, funniest, brightest people I've ever met is falling apart, and she says it's because she's been sexually harassed."

"I'm not neat or funny or bright." Molly's jaw hardened. "I'm stupid and dumb and I wish I were dead."

"Molly!"

"Oh, never mind. I don't mean that. I don't know what I mean."

Darby glanced at the clock on the wall. "We've got time. Let us help you figure it out."

"Do you mean it?"

"I wouldn't have said it if I didn't mean it."

"We all mean it, Molly," Josh added. He didn't give Kate or Andrew a chance to protest.

"I don't have anyone else to talk to. If I told my folks, they'd absolutely kill me. They were so happy when I got the job at Walters Family Restaurant because the pay and the tips are good. They say it's the only way I'm going to get to college, and if I don't go to college, I'll end up working at places like Walters for the rest of my life." Molly's jaw set stubbornly. "And I *won't* work there any longer than I have to. I won't."

"So somebody at the restaurant is harassing you?"

"Not just somebody. My *boss!*"

"Oh, come on, Molly, he wouldn't . . ." Darby's glare shut Andrew down. "Or maybe he would."

"What's Mr. Walters been doing, Molly?" Darby asked gently.

"It's hard to explain. At first, I thought I was imagining it. Later, I thought maybe I was *asking* for it. He just makes these comments . . ."

"About what?"

"My clothes, my hair, what I'm going to do after I get off work. He always wants to know if I have a date. If I say yes, he asks personal questions about what we're going to do. Sometimes, when we're at the cash register alone, he . . . he *touches* me . . ."

Andrew squirmed on his chair.

"How does he touch you, Molly?"

"He tries to make it seem like an accident. That's why I wasn't even sure he was doing it on purpose for a long time. He'll just reach across me to pick up a pen or order book and . . ." Molly blushed a fiery red, ". . . and his arm will brush across my . . . you know, *there*. Sometimes he'll pass by me really close when there's plenty of room, and he rubs his body along mine. It's as if he can read my mind. Just when I'm about to say something, he quits doing it, and I begin to think I was just imagining it, that I'm losing my mind."

"Oh, Molly . . ." Darby wanted to weep.

"It wasn't until a couple months ago that I was sure of what he was doing. We were in the little room off the kitchen where the water, coffee, tea, napkins, and clean silverware are kept. I was stuffing napkin dispensers, and he was filling filters with coffee." Molly choked, as if she weren't getting enough air. Darby squeezed her fingers.

"He touched me . . . he laid his hand on my . . . my chest—and left it there! It was horrible! I could tell he was waiting for me to say something, to *do* something, but I couldn't. I felt like I was frozen! Finally, someone else came toward the room, and he walked away. After he did that, I just walked to the time clock, punched out, and went home."

"What happened then?"

"Nothing. He never said a word. I got paid for my full hours."

Kate's hands flexed. "Creep."

"What exactly did he say to you, Molly?" Andrew pressed.

"Still doubting, Andrew?"

"I just want to know what he said. Maybe it could be a mistake or—"

"It was no mistake." Molly's voice was grim. "I've asked myself that question dozens of times. I've wondered over and over if I'm wrong. I've asked myself if Mr. Walters was just trying to flatter me. I've wondered if that's how adults actually treat each other. My answers are always the same." Molly paused, and a dark silence enveloped them.

Suddenly the sound of Joshua's fist against the tabletop erupted into the void. "He can't do that!" Fury exploded on Josh's features. "We can't *let* him do that!"

"What do you mean?" Molly asked timorously.

"We've got to put a stop to this, Molly."

"I'm not quitting my job. I need the money."

"What could we do anyway?" Kate asked. "We're just a bunch of high-school kids."

"High-school kids with a cable television station at our disposal. High-school kids who get a ninety second feature story on the Saturday night news every week. High-school kids with a radio show and a column in the local newspaper. We're high-school kids with *bite*, and we're going to use it!"

"No." Molly slapped her palms against the tabletop. "You can't do it."

"We can't *not* do it, Molly. This is big. It's a perfect example of what sexual harassment is all about. You are a woman in a vulnerable position. You need that job. You're scared to lose it. Walters knows that. He also knows that you're probably too timid, shy, or embarrassed to tell anyone what's been going on. He's using you, Molly. He's *abusing* you."

"And think what a great story it would be for *Live!*

From Brentwood High." Kate dared to say what the others had been thinking. "Even though it might be painful for you, think of all the good it would do for the viewers who saw our piece and found out that they weren't alone. There must be other people in Brentwood who've experienced something similar."

"Kate's right. What a story this would make for *Live!* It would be even bigger than the last story! As important as anything on network news—and the story would be *ours!*"

"I'd like to do an exposé on that creep."

Fury fanned their excitement.

"Flash that guy's face all over the screen—"

"No!" Molly burst into tears again. "You'll ruin my life! You'll ruin Mr. Walters' life."

"He deserves it," Kate fumed.

"No. Molly's right." Josh had calmed down. "We can't just splash this story all over Brentwood. We have to think of the ramifications."

"Quit using such big words, Josh," Andrew groused.

"You know what I mean. The consequences of the story might be more than we want to be responsible for."

"What's that supposed to mean?"

"What if Mr. Walters' wife sees him on TV and decides to divorce him?"

"It would serve him right."

"But do *we* want to be the ones who made it happen?"

That stopped Kate for a moment. "I guess not. That would be a pretty creepy feeling."

"Or what if he lost his business?"

"That would serve him right too."

"True. But do we want to be the ones who make it happen?"

"I think we're going to have to talk to Ms. Wright and Gary about this."

"No! You can't tell anyone. I shouldn't have talked to you about it either." Molly's tear-stained face was terrified.

"It's okay, Molly," Darby said. "Don't worry. We just got excited and angry when we heard what Mr. Walters has done to you. But it's your story, and we can't make you do a story on your boss. But you *do* have to talk to someone. If you won't tell your family, then you've got to talk to Ms. Wright and Gary. There are some things that you can't deal with alone."

Molly shook her head stubbornly, and her jaw thrust out in dark determination. "I need that job. I have only two years until I graduate. I can take it until then. Then he won't be able to get to me anymore."

"Are you nuts?" Josh asked bluntly. "You must be, if you think you can put up with this for two more years!"

"What choice do I have? Besides, it can't get much worse."

"I wouldn't count on that." Darby's expression was bleak. "If he's doing this to you now, who is to say that his treatment of you won't get worse? What if he threatens you if you don't do what he asks? What if he takes you into his office and—"

"Don't!" Molly put her hands over her ears, and tears squeezed from beneath her tightly closed lids. "Don't say it! Don't think it!"

"You've already thought it," Darby said softly. "I know you have."

Molly kept shaking her head, eyes closed, tears streaming. "I need this job. I want to go to college. I *need this job.*"

"Molly, there are other jobs, scholarships, financial aid . . ."

"Oh, yeah, right. For me? Scholarships? No way. You know my grades aren't good enough to earn all the scholarship aid I'd need. And who wants to graduate from college owing her entire tuition? Besides, how can I be sure I won't get another boss like Mr. Walters?" Molly lifted her chin defiantly. "The pay is good, the tips are the best around, and I'm not going to work twice as many hours for half the income. I'll stick it out. Some days I can avoid Walters entirely. That's what I'll do. Avoid him."

"He's your boss, Molly, you can't avoid him forever."

"No, but I'll try for the next two years." Her brave veneer faltered. "Don't you see? I *have* to!"

"Molly . . ."

"You all have to swear never to tell anyone what I told you today. Will you? You've got to! If you don't, I might not get to go to college!"

Molly looked as though with one more revelation she might shatter. Fragile as glass, vulnerable as a child, it would not take much to make Molly break.

"So what are we going to do?" Andrew, who'd been silent all this time, inquired as Darby and Kate consoled Molly.

"What I'd *like* to do is punch Walters out," Josh said grimly. "But then I'd be no better than he is."

"You guys are certainly getting riled up," Andrew commented. "It seems to me that maybe this whole thing has been blown a little out of proportion. Molly, are you *sure* you aren't exaggerating just a little?"

"Andrew! How can you even ask that?" Darby stormed.

Andrew shrugged. "My parents own a restaurant. I'm positive nothing like this happens there."

"Are you calling me a liar, Andrew Tremaine?" Molly's fury overrode her despair.

"Not a liar, really. Maybe you just thought this Mr. Walters . . ."

". . . thought he wanted to touch me here . . . and here . . . and here . . ." Molly pointed to parts of her body that made Andrew flush.

"Well, I just thought . . ."

"I hate to say this," Darby began, "but if we bring this story out, others are going to ask the same questions. They make you sound like a jerk, Andrew, but unfortunately you aren't alone."

Andrew scowled, not quite sure if Darby had given him a compliment or a slam.

"We should continue with the story," Darby went on. "I think we should research and write the best story anyone has ever seen about sexual harassment. We don't have to mention Molly or her story directly. There must be other case histories we can study. Still, I think it's important that we do it—more important now than ever, because we know how close this issue is to us. If we can't expose Mr. Walters directly, maybe we can stop some others like him."

"You won't mention either of us by name?" Molly said tremulously. "I'd just die if . . ."

"You can have final say on the script and editing. But don't expect us to be too careful. We want this story to be hard-hitting, to mean something."

"And you won't tell anyone else?"

"We won't say a thing—as long as you promise to talk to Ms. Wright or Gary."

"I can't!"

"Then one of us will."

"No. Please . . ."

"I mean it, Molly." Darby was firm. Josh nodded in agreement.

"Then you have to give me some time. I can't just blurt it out. I need to think about how I'll say it."

"Don't take too long, Molly."

"Just a little time . . ."

The door swung open, and Ms. Wright entered in a swirl of perfume. "Sorry that took so long. I'm trying to order some equipment, and it's much more complicated than I thought. I'll have to have Gary—" She stared at all the forlorn faces. "What's wrong?"

Kate and Andrew dived for their books. "Gotta go. W-we're done now, right?" Andrew stammered. They were out the door before anyone had time to answer, leaving Darby, Josh, and Molly behind.

Awkwardly, Josh shifted from one foot to the other before backing toward the table for his books. "I-I promised to talk to Coach Lane before . . . before I left," he sputtered. "I'm late." With a scoop of his hands, he had his books under his arm and was gone.

Ms. Wright looked from Molly to Darby and back again, her astute eyes taking in the scene before her. "Sorry I missed your meeting. Did you get things settled?"

"Settled?" Darby echoed.

"Do you have a plan?"

"Oh, yeah. We'll take care of it. Research and interviews . . ." Darby's voice trailed away.

"Girls, is there anything either of you would like to tell me?"

Molly shot Darby a horrified look. "*No.*"

"I want you to know that if there is ever *anything* either of you or anyone else in the group would like to talk about, I'm here." She smiled faintly. "I've even been told I'm a good listener."

She glanced at Molly's tear-stained face. "In fact, I'm pretty much unshockable. Working in TV has made me that way. Gary too. There's not much that people can do that surprises either of us anymore."

Molly remained silent. She gave Darby a pleading glance. *Don't say anything. I'm not ready. Not now. Not yet.*

"I still think it's a dumb idea. We need a different topic. Maybe sexual harassment exists, but you can't tell me it's all that commonplace."

Andrew, Kate, and Darby were alone in the media room discussing their strategy on the upcoming story—the story that Andrew was still doubtful existed.

"Quit looking at me like that!" He returned the glares Kate and Darby were sending him. "This is a free country! I have a right to express my opinion too, you know."

"The founding fathers probably didn't count on someone as pigheaded as you!" Kate retorted. "How can you doubt for a minute that sexual harassment exists after seeing Molly, after hearing her cry?"

"I didn't say it didn't happen to her. I just said I don't think it's as common as ..." Andrew paused as Molly, Izzy, Jake, and Sarah entered the room. Claudia Webber, one of the seniors who worked part time in the school administration office, followed them in with a folder, which she laid on Ms. Wright's desk.

Sarah had a ribbon in her hair and matching ones braided through the spokes on her wheelchair. Izzy, as he did so often, wore faded jeans, a tattered T-shirt, and a faded flannel shirt. The tails of the shirt flapped around his hips.

Jake moved directly to the table where the others were sitting. "You look serious. Problems with your story?"

"More like problems with our *team*." Kate scowled at Andrew before turning to Jake. "Tell me, do all of you believe that sexual harassment exists?"

"Sure."

"Of course."

"And I think it happens more than any of us realize," Sarah added. "It's the kind of subject we don't like to talk about or to admit having experienced, but we might be surprised if we knew just how many of our friends and family have had a brush with it. I read that last night in one of my mom's women's magazines."

"And that convinced you?" Andrew still sounded doubtful. "I can hardly believe you'd buy into one story in one magazine!"

"Ahem . . ." Claudia cleared her throat. She flushed as everyone turned to stare at her. "I don't mean to interrupt, but what are you talking about?"

"Sexual harassment is our team's research topic for *Live!* Problem is," and Kate frowned at Andrew, "not every one of us believes it actually exists."

"Oh, it exists all right." There was a sharp edge to Claudia's tone.

Darby straightened, her newly emerging reporter's instincts on alert."Why do you say that?"

"Let's just say I've been there. That kind of harassment happens all the time. People don't talk about it, that's all. I'm *glad* you're doing a story on it. I'll be watching for it." Claudia turned to go.

"Wait!" Claudia turned around at Molly's outburst. "Can you tell us more? . . . for the story."

"I quit my first job because of it," Claudia said frankly. "I was always getting mauled by the boss. He acted like it was some big joke and that's what I was there for, to be his little toy. He thought it was funny, but I didn't. He couldn't keep his hands off me. When I complained, he said he was just trying to be 'friendly.'"

"What did you do?"

"Told him to shove off, and then I quit. And he had the nerve to act surprised when I did!" Claudia's pretty features hardened. "There was no way I was going to take it. It was difficult, but I'm glad I stood up for myself. I couldn't work anyway, while I was always looking over my shoulder, wondering when he'd sneak up and try to put his hands on me again."

"What if he *was* just trying to be friendly?" Molly's question was so soft the others had to strain to hear it.

"Are you kidding? The way he behaved was *sick*. I'm glad I told him off." Claudia glanced at her watch. "Gotta go. I think it's great that you're doing a story on this topic. A lot of my friends have had similar things happen to them. It will be good to get it out in the open." With that, she left the room.

Andrew looked sheepish as the girls stared at him. "Okay, so it's a *little* more common than I thought. That still doesn't mean there's someone waiting to harass you around every door!"

"Harassment can take a lot of forms," Josh said softly. "It doesn't have to be physical. I've been harassed verbally because of my color, and it hurts plenty."

"But what could a guy say to a girl that would upset her that much?" Andrew persisted stubbornly in spite of the group's opposing opinion. "Guys say a lot of stuff to girls right here in the hallways at Brentwood. Girls must be used to hearing all that dumb stuff!"

"The 'tongue is like a sharp razor,'" Sarah softly quoted. "It says so in the Psalms. Words can cut your spirit as deeply as a knife can cut into your body."

"I agree with Sarah. Besides, just because you are forced to listen to something because you have to walk down that hallway doesn't mean it's right."

Andrew scowled and punched his fists deep into his pockets, as frustrated and irritated as the rest of them. "You guys just don't understand what I'm saying. Lighten up! So what if people goof around at work or in the halls at school? No one gets hurt. You've got to learn to give and take a little."

"I hear what you're saying, Andrew," Jake commented, "and I understand ... to a point. What *you* don't understand is how much this type of behavior can injure someone." An angry flush ran from beneath Jake's collar and stained his neck. "I might have still thought like you if my sister hadn't been sexually harassed."

"Really?" Kate looked interested. "There's another source for our feature. Would she talk to us about it?"

"I don't know. She was really traumatized for a long time, and it was difficult for her to discuss what had occurred. It's her story to tell, not mine, but I can tell you this, it tore up our whole family until the problem was resolved. It hurt us all."

"My mom had a problem once," Izzy offered. "She was a kindergarten teacher in a big school district. Her principal was always coming into her room to 'observe' her class. That would have been okay with Mom if he'd 'observed' all the other teachers as well, but he didn't. Pretty soon he started coming every day. Then, he kept asking her to come into the hall to discuss one thing or another. When he finally told Mom that if she wanted to get a good evaluation from him, she'd have to go out with him on a date, she got really angry and told him to get lost."

"Then what happened?"

"He did what he promised. He gave her a crummy evaluation and recommended that her contract not be renewed."

"No kidding?"

"Mom fought it. She went to his superior and told her what was going on. Mom found other teachers to back her up, to tell how the principal had been spending too much time in Mom's classroom. One had even over-heard that threatening conversation in the hallway."

"So? Then what?"

"The principal was asked to leave the school system."

"And your mom?"

"She quit too."

"Why? She didn't do anything wrong!"

"No, but she didn't have any heart for working where things like that could happen. Besides, she felt like there were still a few people who thought she did the wrong thing by fighting back. Those people said the principal was good in his job. Some thought Mom hurt the school system by complaining."

"How stupid!"

"That's what she thought. That's also why Mom runs a day care out of her home. She wants to be her own boss and to never have to answer to anyone else, ever again."

"There! That proves it! Sexual harassment is everywhere. If it could affect Izzy's mom, it could affect anyone."

"I don't know..." Andrew's protest was weakening. "I still think that everybody's being a little too sensitive and uptight. I'm not saying Izzy's mom was exaggerating or anything, but..."

"Good. I'm glad you're not saying that," Izzy growled, "because if you were, I'd have to punch you out."

Andrew closed his mouth and sat down.

With Andrew effectively shut up, the others threw themselves enthusiastically into the story.

"I think we need to start interviewing people," Kate announced. "We need to talk to our peers and to hear what they have to say. After all, the story is aimed at them."

"And we should talk to kids in middle school and even grade school," Josh suggested. "We need to know what's happening out there, what they've experienced. We need a wider sampling, a bigger slice of the pie, in order to show the true picture about sexual harassment."

"True," Darby added. "And we'll need all of that evidence to convince Andrew that we're right and he's wrong."

Andrew was about to protest when Darby held up her hand. "It's okay, Andrew. We don't expect everyone to agree on everything. Besides, it might be all right to have a cynic in the group. You'll keep us on our toes. That's good." She turned to the others. "Right?"

She ignored their unenthusiastic response. "Maybe we'd better talk to Gary. He'll have to help us tape the interviews."

"Do you think anyone will talk to us on tape?" Josh wondered. "It's one thing to tell someone privately that you've been harassed, but it's quite another to go on TV and announce it to the world."

"Josh is right. We have to think of people's privacy. What if they're afraid?" It was the first thing Molly had said in a long while.

"What about using distortion techniques for the audio—some sort of unnatural alteration of the voice of the person being interviewed?" Jake asked. "Or blocking out faces on the screen with those big blue dots? Just because someone talked to you wouldn't mean you'd have to reveal their identity. That happens on TV talk shows all the time!"

"Jake's right! What a great idea! Gary must know how to do that. He could teach us."

"I don't know . . ." Molly said, unconvinced.

"Or disguises! The people you interview could wear disguises—wigs, hats, sunglasses . . ."

"Oh, Izzy, grow up!"

"No way."

"We don't want our story to look like it was done at a clown convention."

"Bad idea, Izz."

"So, be glad I'm not on your team this time. I think costumes are a *great* idea."

Even as he spoke, Darby and the others could tell

that Izzy's heart was not in what he was saying. His gaze kept darting to the books he'd left lying on the table nearby.

"What's up with you, Izz-man?" Jake asked. "You aren't going to *argue*? Are you feeling okay?"

"Huh?" Izzy looked up with a befuddled expression on his face. "What did you say?"

"You aren't even listening to us! What's wrong?"

"Oh, nothing, I guess. I was just thinking about what I'm working on for the *Live!* newscast. I might also do a story on the topic for the 'TeenSpeak' column."

"It must be pretty interesting to zone you out like that. What is it?"

"I'm researching the unique new businesses that have been springing up around Brentwood."

Kate wrinkled her pert little nose. "What 'new businesses'? Brentwood is too boring to have new businesses!" Kate pronounced practically everything "boring."

"No, it isn't. In fact, Brentwood is growing fast. Part of the proof of that is the number of businesses that have opened their doors in the last six months. I'm just focusing on the one-of-a-kind, unique ones."

"Like what?"

"A funeral parlor for pets."

"Eee . . . ew! Weird!"

"A bakery that makes only specialty cakes."

"That's a good idea."

"And a tattoo parlor."

"No kidding? I don't even know anyone with a tattoo! There's a tattoo parlor here in Brentwood?"

Izzy brightened. "Great, isn't it?"

"I don't see what's so great about it," Kate huffed. "Who wants to have ugly pictures permanently drawn on their body? Not me."

"They aren't so bad," Izzy retorted. "In fact, I've learned that tattoos have in the past had a lot of historical significance."

"Hah! Like what?" Andrew challenged.

"During the Civil War, and again in the Spanish-American War, soldiers used tattoos to show their loyalty and devotion to their country. Later, a lot of military men got tattooed because it was expected of them by their platoons."

"The 'macho' thing to do, right?"

"It was a way of showing that they'd served their country."

"I don't know, Izzy. It still sounds pretty creepy to me."

"It's not creepy. I think it's neat. The new place here in Brentwood specializes in 'original skin art, photo-realism, body murals, and collages.' They're expecting business from doctors, lawyers, and other professionals—like our parents!"

"If my dad got a tattoo I'd die!" Kate announced. "I'd be ashamed to let him come to school with me. Someone might see it and think he was a sleazeball or something."

"Beauty is in the eye of the beholder," Josh commented. "Someone who gets a tattoo must *like* it. Otherwise, why would they bother to get one?"

"I've always been fascinated by them." Izzy continued bravely, despite the looks of disbelief and dismay around him. "When I see a tattoo, I think the guy wearing it must be really tough—the rugged individualist type. Tattoos aren't for everyone."

"That's for sure." Darby made a face and shuddered. "Although . . . I did see a girl with a little tiny rose tattooed on her shoulder once, and it *did* look kind of neat."

"And some ladies tattoo on permanent eyebrows and eye liner," Kate said. "My mom had a friend who did that once."

"I saw a guy on television who had his entire body tattooed. There was hardly any plain skin left on him, just pictures of snakes, daggers, hearts . . ."

"Just think about taking a shower," Jake said with a laugh. "How'd he know when he was clean?"

"Sounds like he should have been in the circus."

"Actually, tattooed ladies were popular in sideshows before the turn of the century."

"And that's where tattoos should stay—not on you, Izzy!"

"You guys are too much!" Kate spluttered. "We're supposed to be working on our story on harassment, and you all want to talk about Izzy's dumb tattoos! I think we'd better start researching something *important* and leave the goofy stuff to Izzy!"

"Hey! What's that supposed to mean?" Izzy demanded.

"Nothing. It's just that a discussion that jumps from sexual harassment to tattoos in one breath is too much for me. Why can't we focus on one thing at a time?"

"That's what we *like* about television, Kate!" Darby pointed out. "That's what's fun about working in this medium. We *can* jump from one topic to the next. We *can* research whatever we want because there probably is a place for it. Television is a wide-open door. We can work on any topic. We can be serious and attempt to inform and educate, or we can have a little fun and do a story that's pure entertainment."

"And if we don't get to our next class," Sarah reminded them pragmatically as the bell rang, "and educate *ourselves*, we aren't going to even be working in this program any longer."

That was warning enough. *Live! From Brentwood High* had already become too important to all of them to jeopardize their place in the program now. Chaos Central emptied within seconds.

———

"Did you hear about Gerilyn?" Kate demanded as Darby walked into the media room. Kate was excited. Her dark eyes glittered and her silky black hair swung around her face.

"The girl whose name is written in the boys' locker room?"

"Yes. I talked to her today." Kate flushed at Darby's look of surprise. "It was worth a shot. I thought she might be willing to talk to us about what's been happening."

"You didn't! Gerilyn is so shy I can't imagine her talking to anyone."

"I know, but I had to ask."

"What did she say?"

"More than I expected she would. I think she was so frustrated that she just couldn't keep it inside anymore. She told me her parents called the school counselor to talk about what's happened."

"And?"

"And they promised to 'check it out.' Then, just as

her dad was about to hang up, the counselor said, 'You know, Mr. McDonald, this is the sort of thing that usually goes away if it's ignored; after all, boys will be boys.' "

"You're kidding!"

"Gerilyn broke down just talking about it. How humiliating! What's she supposed to do? Walk into the locker room and paint over all the graffiti herself? I don't think she's ever been strong on self-esteem, but whatever she had is in shreds now.

"And that's not all! Just wait until you hear this!" Kate waved a sheaf of papers under Darby's nose. "You won't believe it! According to the studies I read, over three-fourths of all high-school girls and half of all high-school boys have experienced sexual looks or comments. They also reported touching, grabbing, pinching, as well as having their clothes pulled at, pornographic materials thrust on them . . ."

With a theatrical flair, Kate began to spout the facts and figures she'd compiled. As Kate read, Molly withdrew into the tight, invisible shell she'd constructed around herself lately. Her face grew pinched and tense, her gaze restless.

Across the room, Andrew was having an entirely different reaction to Kate's information.

"Where'd you get those figures? If you didn't get them from the library, you can't count on them being correct. Has Ms. Wright looked at this?"

"I did all my research on the computer in the library, Andrew. I didn't make any of it up, if that's what you're implying."

"Give her a break," Shane growled from a nearby table. "Maybe you'll have to admit for once that you were wrong and someone else was right."

Kate was obviously surprised that Shane had come to her defense. He spoke so little and so seldom that it was easy to forget that he, too, might have an interest in what this report uncovered.

"While you were in the library, I was in phys. ed.," Darby said. She waved her own stack of papers in the air. "I've already got a list of girls who have agreed to be interviewed on the topic. I explained what we were doing and put out a sign-up sheet. It was full before class started."

"I didn't think that many people would agree to be interviewed."

"I told them that even if they were willing to talk to us, they could remain anonymous. Some didn't care. They said they didn't mind being on TV. Others said they'd do it only if they didn't have to give their identities."

Darby turned to Gary, who was tinkering with his camera. "We can make that work, can't we?"

Gary nodded. "We can always tape the interviewees in shadow, I suppose. Or, better yet, we can use a mosaic effect."

"What's that?"

"The images of the people you're interviewing can be broken down into squares of equal size but of different brightness and color. You've seen it done on news magazine shows, I'm sure. The face of the interviewee looks more like a graphic image than a human face. A mosaic is a digitally constructed image. Don't worry. It sounds more difficult than it is. We'll cover it in class."

While Darby and Gary were talking, Shane moved

across the room to where Darby sat. Quietly, he picked up her list of volunteers.

Shane was slender but muscular. His sleek, strong build spoke of grace and agility. Though he had never participated in organized sports, Shane spent a lot of time alone in the weight room working out. He usually kept everyone at a distance and rarely encouraged conversation.

His hair was a dark blond color—golden with streaks of brown and near black. He scraped a long, straight lock of hair out of his eye as he looked up from the list he was reading. "These are all girls."

"So? That's usually who's in girls' phys. ed."

"What makes you think that sexual harassment is purely a female problem?"

The media room grew very quiet. Even Gary stopped handling his camera and looked curiously toward Darby and Shane.

"Do you think that happens?" Darby asked.

"Why not? You aren't going to give a very clear picture of harassment if you don't ask."

Shane's statement stopped everyone cold for a moment. He had surprised them all.

"Do you have any suggestions who we should contact?" Darby asked, but Shane had already closed down again. That aloof protective shell surrounded him.

"Don't clam up now, Shane! You've given us a good idea. Now help us out!"

"He's not saying anything because he doesn't *know* anything! He's just trying to get you all excited," Andrew scoffed. "Men being sexually harassed? Get real!"

"You don't think it's possible?"

"For a few wimps, maybe, but not for real *men*."

"Are you sure?" Gary inquired softly, surprising them all. He rarely interrupted their conversations. "Are you *sure*?"

"Guys can handle that sort of thing!" Andrew said.

"Can they?"

Something in Gary's tone caused them all to pause and consider his question.

"Maybe we should interview guys too."

"It would be easy to get volunteers from both middle and grade schools. So what if it's a few more people to talk to? We do need to offer a complete picture."

"We might as well be thorough."

At that moment, Molly slammed her books to her desk and stood up. "I'm sick and tired of this conversation! Can't you people ever talk about anything else?" With that, she walked out of the room.

CHAPTER 5

LIVE

FROM DRENTWOOD HIGH

"Are we ready?" Darby whispered to Jake as he peered through the viewfinder of a studio camera at the set they had put together for the upcoming interviews. The viewfinder was nothing more than a small monochrome—black-and-white—television set mounted on the camera that allowed Jake to see what the camera was "seeing."

"Almost. Have they started to arrive yet?" He referred to the students who had agreed to be interviewed.

"Any minute." Darby grabbed at her stomach. "Why am I so nervous?"

"Because you've never done this before?"

At that moment, Andrew stalked through the studio with a sour expression on his face.

"What's with him?" Jake wondered.

"Didn't you hear about the big uproar?" Darby asked. "Everyone was hoping to be chosen to do the on-camera interviews, but Andrew insisted that *he* was the one who should be doing them."

"That's no surprise. Andrew likes to see himself on screen."

"Exactly. He forgot, however, that an interviewer

needs *questions* and *preparation*. He assumed that Ms. Wright would choose him because of his pretty face. He had a fit when she chose Josh to interview the guys and me to interview the girls."

"No wonder he's crabby."

"That's not the end of it. He complained so loudly that Ms. Wright agreed to reconsider as long as Andrew turned in his prepared list of questions within an hour."

"And?"

"And he had no questions. No preparation. Nothing. He'd planned to get in front of the camera and wing it."

"And he's the one guy who thinks this story is garbage to begin with!"

"Exactly. What he got from Ms. Wright was a big lecture about being poorly prepared and having a 'destructive' attitude." Darby grimaced. "It was embarrassing!"

Jake shook his head and chuckled. "I'm glad this is your story and not mine." He took one more glimpse through the viewfinder. "The set looks good. I think you're ready. By the way, why did Ms. Wright decide to have two interviewers instead of just one?"

"She felt that since we were asking questions of such a personal, private nature that same-sex reporters would make it more comfortable for the volunteers."

"She thinks of everything, doesn't she?" Jake commented with respect in his voice.

"Between her and Gary, nothing gets missed," Darby agreed.

Kate came by muttering to herself and interrupted their conversation. "I never realized there was so much to think about. Camera angles, lighting, sound, patching, switching . . ."

" . . . itching, twitching." Izzy finished for her as he loped up behind her and drew one of Kate's famous glares.

Ms. Wright strode into the center of the melee and cleared her throat. "I want to run over a few things before we begin taping. Josh, Darby, take special note. You are television performers today. I don't mean that you're actors, but performers. Part of your job is to sell yourself to the audience. You'll be doing some heavy-duty interviews, and you'll want to come across as sincere, believable, and reliable.

"Imagine that you're talking, not to three hundred students in the lunchroom or every person in 'video land,' but to a few intimate acquaintances who've gathered around a television set to get some information about your topic. Be aware of your guests' comfort. This isn't an easy topic to discuss. Help them out. Show them your compassion, your interest, and your concern.

"Keep in mind that the camera is watching you. It won't turn politely away if you yawn or pick your nose. Therefore, it's up to you, Darby and Josh, to exhibit some self-control. Don't twitch or itch or squirm. The camera will catch you."

Darby and Josh exchanged an uncomfortable glance.

"Look into the lens during your introductions. That is your audience. It is imperative that you establish eye contact with your viewer."

"All the time?" Josh wondered. "Can't we look away for even a second?"

"It's best if you don't. The television screen intensifies your every move. Glancing away breaks the connection between you and your audience. That reminds the audience that they are just watching a television show, not communicating directly with you. How would you like it if Tom Brokaw kept glancing away when he was reading the evening news?"

"Okay . . ." Josh looked worried.

Gary ambled over to him and grinned. "Don't worry. We're only going to use one camera today so you don't have to worry about which one is 'hot' or need to be cued to a second camera. Just go for it. You'll be fine."

"The first guest is ready." Molly stuck her head into the studio. "I've briefed her and gone over some of the questions you'll be asking. Can I send her in?"

A tall, slender girl of seventeen walked into the studio amidst a flurry of activity. Darby invited her to the set and asked her to sit down.

"I'm going to fasten a microphone on your lapel," Darby explained. "Once it's attached, you can forget about it. Let the audio engineer worry about the sound. My name is Darby Ellison, and I'll be conducting this interview. You are . . ."

"Helen Jensen." Helen's voice was soft. Darby hoped that they'd be able to pick it up in the sound booth.

"Okay, Helen, do you have any questions for me before we get started?"

Helen shook her head. Darby wondered if she could manage to get more than a word or two out of this shy girl. Why had she agreed to this interview in the first place?

"I'm speaking today with Helen Jensen, a senior at

Brentwood High School. Today on *Live! From Brentwood High* we're discussing sexual harassment—is it fact or fantasy here at Brentwood?"

Darby turned to her guest. "Helen, there's been a lot of discussion nationwide about the prevalence of sexual harassment in the workplace. How about here in school or in the places teenagers work?"

Helen sat quietly for a moment, as if gathering her courage. When she looked into the camera her eyes were clear, her voice steady.

"Oh, it's here, all right. You just don't hear people talk about it much. It's painful and it's embarrassing. That's why I agreed to be interviewed. It's time *somebody* started talking."

Darby felt a throb of excitement at Helen's answer. This was exactly what she was hoping for!

"Why do you think people are so reluctant to discuss being harassed?"

"They're scared. They're afraid it's their own fault. I think kids are harassed because they are young and inexperienced and somehow convinced that they've asked for it. I was harassed by an older co-worker at my first job, and I would have died before telling anyone what was happening." Helen began to warm to her subject.

"I suppose I acted pretty cool, because no one seemed to notice that anything was wrong." Helen gave a bitter laugh. "I might have looked like I was doing all right, but I was coming apart inside."

"Would you have accepted help had someone offered it?"

"Yes! But everyone acted as though I *liked* having this guy put his hands on me and say rude, insinuating things about me." Helen's lower lip trembled. "The people I worked with were afraid to speak up. They didn't want to interfere because it might cause trouble for them. That's why I wanted to come to *Live!* today. To tell everyone that if they know someone is being harassed—particularly a teenager—it's their job to *say something.*

"It's funny," Helen continued, almost unaware of the rolling camera or the silent, interested eyes of the *Live!* crew upon her. "But I was really *glad* to see that sign-up sheet in phys. ed. the other day. It feels good to know that you aren't alone with your problem; that it's real. There must be others who've been harassed if it's important enough to do a television show about, right?"

Darby nodded but did not interrupt.

"I've thought about my boss's hateful little remarks so long that it actually feels good to know that others know what I've gone through. Just seeing that sheet and hearing that you thought this was an important story was like having a friend reach out and tell me that I wasn't alone anymore."

Darby remained silent, her prepared questions unasked. Helen had her own story to tell. Darby could sense from the rapt attention of the crew that what they were filming was very powerful.

"My parents made me quit my job when I got an ulcer. At first they thought I was working too hard—having a job, homework, school activities. When I finally told them what was really wrong, they really spazzed. I'm glad I wasn't depending on that job to support a family or anything. What would I have done

then? Kept on working and feeling ashamed and dirty?
I suppose so."

"What would you advise others to do who find themselves in similar situations?" Darby leaned forward in
her chair, willing away the tenseness she felt in her
body, knowing the camera would pick up every nuance
of her behavior.

"Go to your parents. Tell someone what's happening
to you. Ask for the help of a counselor who can give you
a new perspective on what's happening to your life.
Please."

Everyone was silent after Darby wrapped up her
interview with Helen. Even Andrew was left speech-
less.

After Helen left the room with Ms. Wright, Darby
turned to Gary. "I feel wiped out."

"Me too, and I was behind the camera. Good job,
Darb."

"I didn't do anything. I just opened the floodgate
and the story came rushing out."

"Anybody still got any ideas about this not being an
important story?" Gary asked casually, his eyes on Andrew.

Andrew refused to look up.

"Your next interviewees are here and have already
been prepped," Molly announced as she led three
young teenage girls into the studio. "Here are Tanya,
Mary, and Jessica. They said you'd agreed to interview
them together."

"Great. Come on up here and we'll get going."
Darby waved a hand to indicate chairs for the girls. The
girls, all dressed in jeans and sweatshirts, trooped onto

the set and took their places with a trill of nervous giggles.

"It's really neat to get out of class to do this," one announced.

"Yeah. And to be on TV too!"

"Do you all understand the topic of this program?" Darby inquired as she attached the third mircrophone. After the great emotion Helen had shown, these younger girls didn't seem prepared for what the interview might bring.

"Oh, sure. We know all about sexual harassment!"

Shane, acting as floor manager—the link between Darby and the director—gave a nonverbal cue to begin taping while the girls were still chatting animatedly.

"Would you tell me what you know?" Darby asked.

"Are we on TV now?" the little redhead demanded. Darby nodded.

"Oh, okay, then." She peered toward the camera. "What do you want to know?"

"She wants to know if we really know what it means!" the girl named Mary interjected.

"Sexual harassment is uninvited and unwelcome sexual behavior that bothers, frightens, or hurts you," Tanya quoted. "That's what we learned in health class."

"And has that happened to you?"

"Oh, sure. The day I was collecting class dues, this guy stuck his money—and his hand—down the front of my shirt! Another time, the same guy put his foot on the hem of my skirt while I was sitting down. When I stood up, the skirt was pulled right down to my knees."

"And people are always saying rude, crude things in the hallways or trying to touch and pinch and grab at you. It's sick."

Tanya straightened indignantly. "Once I found a dirty magazine full of naked people in my locker. I almost got in trouble for having it there, but the principal believed me when I told him it wasn't mine. He caught the kids who put it there, but all they had to do was stay after school."

"What do you do when this happens to you?"

"Ignore it. Try to pretend it doesn't 'get' to you. Otherwise, it encourages those people to do it again."

"Besides," Mary concluded, "it happens all the time at school. Most people think you're overreacting if you make a big deal over something like getting brushed up against in the hall.

"One day we found out that someone had drilled a hole into the wall of our locker room. They'd been spying on us while we were taking showers!"

"It makes me *mad*," Tanya said. "Really mad. And it hurts. But I don't know what to do about it."

"How do you feel, Jessica?"

"The same way Tanya does." Jessica looked down at the floor and wove her fingers nervously together. "And I feel embarrassed . . . and cheap."

"Cheap?" Darby echoed.

"Yeah. Like the people who do that to me don't care about me as a person. I'm just a . . . thing . . . to them, a thing to be teased and laughed at. And I'm *not* a thing. I'm a *person*!"

The emotion that erupted from the three girls surprised Darby. They'd seemed so carefree and happy-go-lucky. Who could have known the pain they were hiding?

"When I get harassed at school, I feel self-conscious for the rest of the day. I worry about how I look. Maybe my clothes weren't right and I stood out in the crowd. Maybe I'm too fat or too ugly. I don't know." Tears flooded Jessica's eyes. "I try all the time to fit in, but sometimes it just doesn't work out."

————

"I'm exhausted." Darby leaned back in her chair after Tanya, Mary, and Jessica had departed. "I didn't realize how emotionally draining this would be."

"One more interview to go and then Josh will take over," Gary said. "Think of it this way—you have some very powerful footage."

"Editing this is going to be hard," Josh commented. "There's nothing that's been said so far that I want to cut out."

"No time to rest." Molly stepped into the room. "Here's interview number three."

Hayley Barnes walked into the studio with the air of an injured puppy. She appeared hurt, timid, and a very poor candidate for an interview.

"Hayley? I'm Darby. Welcome to *Live! From Brentwood High*."

"They promised me that if I talked to you, my identity would be kept anonymous. Is that right?"

"Yes. We have techniques for distorting your voice and image if you'd like."

"Good. I don't want him to know I talked to you."

"Him?"

Hayley's lips pressed into a grim line. "My ex-boyfriend."

"Let's get comfortable on the set, Hayley," Darby encouraged. "Then I'd like to have you tell me all about it."

The story that spilled from Hayley stunned them all.

"I'm an honor student . . . at least I *was*, before all this happened." Her blue eyes filled with tears. "I thought that meeting Ted—that's not his real name, but it's the one I'll use—I thought that Ted was the perfect completion to my junior year of high school. He's tall, good-looking, rich—everything I thought a guy should be. Until I decided to break up with him, that is."

"What made you decide to do that?"

"Ted was really possessive." Hayley frowned. "At first it was flattering, but then he became totally jealous. He'd yell at me for *looking* at some other guy in class or for talking to the boy whose locker is next to mine! Sometimes he'd push me around a little. I didn't like it, but I didn't want to lose him, so I never said anything. Then he pushed me too hard, and I fell down and hit my head. I needed three stitches. My parents were furious. They said I should get rid of Ted immediately. By that time, I agreed with them. That's when the real trouble started."

"The harassment?" Darby noticed out of the corner of her eye that there was a flurry of activity in the sound room. She hoped nothing would break Hayley's concentration.

"He started calling me filthy names when he saw me at the mall or in the hallways at school. Sometimes he'd throw food at me in the cafeteria or pretend he'd tripped and would spill milk or juice all over me.

"I heard from a friend of a friend that he'd been saying all sorts of things about what we'd done together— sexual things that I'd *never* do until I was married.

"He was even bold enough to put his hands on me and rub against me in the hallways at school."

"And you let him?"

"He's big. Nearly six foot four. And strong. I couldn't forget how he'd pushed me around. I was sure that if I fought back, he'd hurt me."

Hayley's lip trembled. "It sounds really dumb now, but at the time, I couldn't think of anything else. I was terrified that Ted would catch me sometime when I was alone and . . ." Her voice trailed away. Everyone in the room knew exactly what she was thinking.

"I started skipping school. It was the only way I could avoid him because he was in three of my classes. I ended up failing one class and getting *D*'s in the others. Now my hopes for a scholarship are history. Ted's ruined my life."

"Where is he now?"

"He graduated last spring. I suppose he's tormenting some other innocent victim at a college somewhere." Hayley looked at Darby with tear-filled eyes. "That's why I volunteered to be interviewed. Until people start talking about sexual harassment and doing something about it, it's going to continue. I don't want anyone else's life ruined—mine was enough."

Everyone was somber as they went through the motions of wrapping up the interview. When Darby returned to the studio after walking Hayley to the door, she came face-to-face with Andrew.

"Well, Andrew, what do you think?" She looked intently into his eyes.

"You were right and I was wrong," Andrew said, looking for the first time genuinely contrite. "Sexual harassment exists. Even I'm convinced."

CHAPTER 6

LIVE

FROM BRENTWOOD HIGH

Darby met Josh in the hallway after his taping was complete. He looked worn out.

"How'd it go? I'm sorry I had to sneak out, but I had one more rehearsal to fit in before our concert on Saturday." Darby referred to a vocal performance class in which she was involved. The group occasionally performed for local functions around Brentwood.

"Fine. Great, actually, if you can call the kinds of things those boys said 'great.'" Josh leaned heavily against the wall and pulled at the collar of his shirt. "I'm whipped. I didn't realize how emotionally involved I'd get with this thing.

"It never occurred to me that sexual harassment could be as big a problem for boys as for girls." Josh shook his head in disbelief. "I'm glad Shane said something. Their stories nearly blew me away."

"Tell me about it."

"They expressed very similar problems to those girls have. They complained of girls pinching them or slapping them on the rear when they walk past. Some said they'd had girls announce to everyone within hearing distance all the rude, lewd things they wanted to do to a guy. Sometimes girls started stories about things she'd done with a certain guy—and none of it was true."

"How stupid!"

"What's wrong with our society, Darby?" Josh wondered. "Why do people feel free to do things like that to one another?"

"Sarah and I talked about that the other day. I asked her the same question because I was so *frustrated* by what I've learned researching this story. She had a pretty interesting comment. She said that we behave the way we do—rude, thoughtless, hurtful— because of sin."

"That sounds like Sarah. Is she talking about church things again?"

"It's more than just a 'church thing' with her. Sarah really lives what she believes. The better I get to know her, the more I think that she's on to something. Think about it, Josh. For a lot of people, it's easier to be mean or crude or thoughtless than it is to be kind, generous, or gentle. It's as though our first instinct is to be a creep. That's what Sarah means by sin."

"If *none* of us can be good because it's not in our nature, then what's the point of trying?"

"We *can* be better, according to Sarah, but it takes help—what she calls 'Heavenly Help.'"

"I'm not much of a churchgoer," Josh muttered, "but I do agree with Sarah that there's a lot of evil in the world. The more we work on this report, the more I'm beginning to see it. What's worse, we've all either observed, experienced, or practiced sexual harassment at some time or other—and probably never even realized it. We certainly haven't spoken out about it like we could have."

"That's a scary thought."

"When I was a kid, some older boys in our neighborhood used to pick on a girl down the street. They'd run up and snap her bra strap or make jerky comments about her figure. She used to cry and run away. One day, I told my grandmother about it. She just shook her head and said, 'Boys will be boys.' I never understood why she ignored the situation, but I suppose the same sort of thing had happened to her as a girl. If society overlooks something long enough, people begin to accept the behavior—whether it is all right or not."

"That's exactly what the school counselor told Gerilyn's parents! He wanted to ignore the problem too." A curious expression flitted across Darby's features. "What did the guys say they did when they were harassed?"

"They tried to ignore it. They all said they tried not to make it a big deal because all their friends acted like they were *lucky* to be the one singled out. They said the message they received from their friends was that they were supposed to *like* it, so they didn't dare protest too loudly even if it made them feel crummy inside.

"Most of them were embarrassed by it—but they were more embarrassed *admitting* their embarrassment. Most wanted to be anonymous. And they all said they'd like the harassment to stop because it didn't feel funny anymore."

"We really opened a can of worms with this story, didn't we?" Darby murmured softly. "Where is it all going to end?"

———

"Break time!" Izzy roared as he glided into the studio wearing a pair of in-line skates and a cowboy hat. Molly, Kate, and Darby looked up from their research while Andrew, Jake, and Shane stared at Izzy from the audio booth. Gary, who was bent over Ms. Wright's desk, straightened.

"I've got Sarah and Julie outside in Sarah's van. We're going blading!"

"There's too much work to do!" Kate complained. "Quit goofing off, Izzy."

"C'mon! School's over already. You're not planning on spending the night here, are you? All work and no play makes Kate ... and Darby ... and Molly ... dull girls. We've been working too hard. It's time to have a little fun. My mom's cousin owns Skateland. He said that if I brought ten people, he'd give us a great discount—and free soda." Izzy did a little dance step on his skates and nearly ended up on his rear end. "What are you all waiting for?"

Jake's voice floated into the room via the public address system. "We're trying to learn how this thing works, Izz. You should be in here too."

"I already know how it works. I read the book last night." Izzy tapped his temple with an index finger. "Photographic memory, remember?"

"Well, none of the rest of us have photographic memories, so we'll have to work at it."

"Wait a minute." Everyone turned to Gary as he spoke. "I think Izzy is right. You've all been working very hard. You deserve a break. You'll come back refreshed and ready to learn. Get out of here—all of you."

"Yes!" Izzy pumped his arm next to his body in a victory gesture. "Thanks, Gary. Want to come along?"

For an instant, he looked as if he might say yes.

Then Gary smiled and shook his head. "Not this time."

"What about Sarah?" Molly asked. "Won't she feel left out while we're skating?"

Izzy looked at her disparagingly. "Are you kidding? Sarah's on wheels all the time! I'm going to push her. We're going to learn to dance." Izzy rolled around the room, pretending to push and twirl Sarah's wheelchair.

Gary threw a pencil in the air. It landed in a potted plant on the windowsill. "I give up. You're nuts. We're *all* nuts! And I think Izzy's right. Let's go skating!"

———

Izzy's outing had provided them all with a much-needed break, but as Darby, Jake, and the others were quickly learning, television was a demanding medium.

"What are *you* doing here?" was Jake's greeting as he walked through the media room door to find Darby and Josh huddled near the television and VCR. Shane was reading a camera manual nearby.

"Working. What else? Even *Shane* came back to study!"

Josh yawned and stretched, arching his body over the seat back. "If I'd realized how much time this media stuff was going to consume, I don't know if I would have applied."

"Do you mean that?"

Josh grinned. "No."

"I thought so." Jake dropped onto a chair beside Darby. "What are you doing?"

"Reviewing some tapes of newscasts. We're studying technique. After seeing ourselves on the interview tapes, both Josh and I decided that we need some improvement."

"You looked good to me."

"Thanks, but what we did won't get either of us a job on the six o'clock news."

"Aren't you being a little hard on yourselves? After all, we just started this program."

"What are *you* doing here?"

Jake blushed. "I'd planned to do the same thing. I've got an interview scheduled for next week, and I didn't want to make a fool of myself."

They were all laughing when Gary Richmond walked through the door. Though they may have been surprised to see one another there, none were surprised to see Gary. The media room and studio seemed to be his second home—or maybe his first. He was always staying late or coming early to tinker with equipment, develop photos, or look through Ms. Wright's impressive collection of books on communications.

Gary had a pizza under one arm and a liter bottle of cola hung between two fingers. In his other hand was one of his ever-present cameras. "I didn't expect anyone to be here" was his greeting.

"Obviously," Josh joked. "That pizza isn't big enough for all of us."

Gary grinned and dropped it onto a nearby table. "No, but I can always order more. Have you had supper?"

"Not yet, but that's all right." Josh looked at Gary curiously. "What are you doing here?"

"There was nothing to do in my apartment," Gary admitted with a shrug. "I thought I'd come here and look through Rosie's library. She's got some great stuff on the early days of radio. Never thought much about radio before, but now that some of you will be working in the medium, I've become interested."

"Sounds like an exciting night."

Gary pinioned Jake with a look. "Are you making fun of my plans for the evening?"

Jake squirmed. "Maybe I was ... just a little. It seems that a guy like you ..."

"What *is* a 'guy like me'?"

"Smart, well-traveled, talented ... single ..."

"You mean why don't I have a date tonight?" A smile tugged at the corners of his lips. "Curious, aren't you?"

Jake blushed but held his ground. He wasn't the only one curious about Gary's life.

Gary dropped into a chair and opened the pizza carton. After he'd lifted out a stringy piece of pepperoni pizza and taken a bite, he glanced at Josh and Darby. They were staring at him with undisguised interest.

"I'm nobody's fool. I know you all wonder why I spend so much time working." He shrugged again. "Can't help it. It's been my way of life since my teens. In the jobs I've had, it's paid to be a nomad, a wanderer. A wife and family would have held me back—prevented me from volunteering for the dangerous assignments. I chose adventure over the safe path. Maybe that was a mistake, but I did it. I don't stay home because there's nothing there for me, that's all."

"Are you sorry sometimes?" Darby asked softly. "Do you wish you could go back and do it all over again?"

Gary thought for a moment before shaking his head. "No. I've lived and seen more than most men ever do.

I've had an exciting life—and I'm not done yet. Sometimes I miss having a wife and kids, but maybe that's why I'm enjoy working with Rosie here at Brentwood High. I get to know what it might be like to have teenagers." He reached into the pizza box. "Are you *sure* none of you wants a slice of this?"

"My dad left us 'cause he didn't want to be tied down," Shane murmured. Four pairs of eyes turned toward him. "Sometimes I think it would have been better if he'd made the decision like you, not to have kids at all."

Jake and Darby exchanged a startled glance. None of them had known this about Shane's family.

Shane studied his fingernails intently. "My mom says that not every man is good at raising a family, but I think that a man should find that out early—before his family is already here."

He looked at the ceiling. "It's not easy growing up without a father. It's harder still to know you have a father *somewhere* and that he just doesn't want to be with you or your mom." Shane lowered his gaze. "I'm not sure what this has to do with anything except that I wanted to say that I respect your decision."

There seemed little to be said after that. Eventually they settled into a comfortable silence, each at the task they'd come to do.

Gary was the first to break the silence with a noisy yawn and a big, graceless stretch. "Are any of you tired of this yet?"

Darby rubbed her eyes with her fists. "I am. So far I've learned that I did practically everything wrong that I could. I could hardly stand to watch our tape. I look like an idiot!"

"No worse than me," Josh assured her. "We're doing this backward. We should have been smart like Jake and studied interviewing techniques *first*."

"Look at it this way: at least you're learning them." Gary rolled his broad shoulders to relax them. "Anybody interested in a cup of coffee or a slice of pie?"

"Why? Do you have some in the pockets of your jacket?"

"No, but if anyone is interested, I'll find us a nearby restaurant."

"Sounds good to me," Jake said. "I might even eat some supper. My parents aren't home, and I'm supposed to cook. That's part of the reason I come here—to avoid the kitchen."

"Count me out," Shane said. "I've got plans." He didn't divulge what they were.

"Let's go." Gary stood up and ushered them toward the door.

"How about Walters Family Restaurant?" Gary asked as they turned out of the parking lot. "It's close, and they have the best pie I've discovered so far."

"Sure. That's where Molly works." Darby and Josh exchanged a glance. It couldn't hurt to check up on Molly, considering the mood she'd been in lately.

As Darby walked through the large glass door into the restaurant, she took a deep breath. What would they find inside?

CHAPTER 7

LIVE
FROM DRENTWOOD HIGH

"Welcome to Walters." A nice-looking woman in her mid-fifties greeted them at the door of the restaurant.

They followed the hostess to a booth directly across from a large doorway that led to the kitchen. On either side of the doorway were cupboards and counters, where ice water, napkins, and beverages were dispensed. Molly and Mr. Walters were working there together, folding flatware into large paper napkins for the tables. Neither noticed the group's arrival.

"Busy place tonight," Gary commented. "I usually don't get stuck in this booth."

"This is fine," Josh blurted so quickly Gary looked at him in surprise. What Josh *really* meant was that it was fine to be near Molly—especially since her boss was near *her*.

They were greeted again by the older woman, who arrived to distribute menus. Gary asked for the dessert menu and ordered coffee—strong and black.

Josh, however, appeared distracted and uninterested in the menu. He kept glancing in Molly's and Mr. Walters' direction. Suddenly he choked on a sip of water, and liquid came spewing out across the table.

"Are you all right?" Gary pounded Josh on the back.

"Yes . . . no!" Josh sputtered. "Did you see what I just saw?" His gaze connected with Darby's.

"What are you talking about?"

"He put his hand on her butt!"

"Huh?" While Gary and Jake stared at Josh as if he'd lost his mind, Darby 's face froze with fear. "Mr. Walters?"

"Mr. Walters!"

"The guy who owns this place?" Gary asked.

"Shhhh . . . he might hear you!"

"What's wrong with you, man?" Jake chided. "Are you losing it? He wouldn't—"

"The guy standing over there folding napkins just reached down and patted Molly's behind! I *saw* it!"

Gary looked skeptical. "Why didn't she stop him? The Molly I know would have punched him in the mouth!"

"Then you don't know Molly very well."

From his vantage point Jake stared at the pair in the enclosure off the kitchen. His eyes widened. "You weren't kidding! When Molly leaned over to put water into glasses on a tray, that guy just moved over and rubbed against her!"

At that moment, Mr. Walters caught sight of the interested, disbelieving stares from the booth and abruptly moved away from Molly. Molly, her cheeks flushed, never looked up.

White knuckled, Gary began to stand. Josh's and Darby's hands shot out to restrain him. When Molly arrived at their table with water glasses on a tray, she was pale, and her hands shook so that the glasses chinked together. She spilled Gary's water as she set it on the table.

"I'm sorry. I'll go get a rag to wipe that up. . . ."

Josh put his hand on Molly's wrist. "Wait. We want to talk to you. What went on back there just now?"

"Nothing. Let go, Josh. I don't want to get yelled at."

"I have eyes, Molly. So does Jake. We both saw him touch you."

Gary listened to the conversation without comment, his lips pressed into a grim line.

"Well, if you 'saw' something, then why ask me about it? If you're so smart, think of the answers for yourself."

"Darby and I just spent hours interviewing people who've had the same kinds of experiences. You can't keep on ignoring it forever."

"Just leave it alone," Molly pleaded. "If he sees us talking like this and thinks you saw him . . . I don't know what might happen. He'll be leaving in a few minutes. Wait until then. Please?"

Molly was on the verge of tears. Terror, fear, and humiliation played on her features.

Josh let go of her arm. "Just till then. After that we're going to talk."

As Molly put the last of the glasses on the table, Mr. Walters sauntered over. He had a jacket draped over his arm. "Evening folks. Is everything okay?"

Gary glanced at Molly before answering. "Fine, thank you. Good, prompt service."

"And could you name all those kinds of pie again?" Darby asked. "I forgot all the types you listed."

The suspicious look on Mr. Walters' face relaxed. "Very good, Miss Ashton. Excuse me, folks, but it's time for me to go. Good-night."

They watched him depart through the side door.

When he was gone, Molly sagged against the table and closed her eyes. A tear leaked from beneath her lids.

"Hey, Molly," someone called from the kitchen. "You want to take your break now or should I?"

"I will. I'll be here with my friends." Molly slid into the booth next to Darby. She was visibly trembling. No one took their eyes off her face.

"You'd better explain that entire scene," Gary finally said. He was calm again, but there was a steely glint in his eyes which signaled that he meant business.

"What is there to tell? You saw it for yourself. He touches me. He tries to get me alone or off to one side when no one is watching. He usually doesn't slip up like that. He tells the hostess to seat this booth last. That's because when there are people seated here, he can't do his little touching games. When you sat down he must have been too busy concentrating on his roaming hands to notice that you'd arrived."

"The others seem to know about this situation, Molly, but I think you'd better fill me in." Gary's words were a command, not a suggestion.

"My boss is the reason I suggested our team do a piece on sexual harassment," Molly whispered fearfully. "I thought that maybe I'd learn what to do about him if we . . ." The tears she'd been holding back flooded down her cheeks.

"What has he done to you?" There was a bridled fury in Gary's voice that none of them had ever heard before.

"Mostly touching." Molly blew her nose on a napkin from the nearby dispenser. "That and making lewd, disgusting sexual comments. He does that all of the time. Then, if someone protests, he says he was 'just kidding' and that we should develop a sense of humor. Sometimes he tells jokes and demonstrates them with these horrible gestures. . . ."

A growl came from deep in Gary's chest.

"I've never dared ask the other girls if he's tried anything with them. He's usually very careful. Tonight was the first time he's ever slipped up."

"No one *says* anything?"

"We all hate him. I don't think he likes women very well, even though he does all this touching and grabbing. He couldn't like women and still treat us like that or tell such horrible jokes . . . could he?"

"Molly, this has to stop." Gary's words were firm.

"But how? He's my boss. I *have* to work here. It's the best tips in town. If I quit now, I'll never save enough for college!"

"I consider this a *dangerous* situation, Molly. If he's bold enough to do these things in a building full of people, who's to say what he might do if he caught you on your way home or alone in the parking lot or in your car?"

Molly paled. "I never thought about that."

"Well, start thinking. You have only two choices: find a way to put a stop to this or quit your job."

"Why doesn't anyone understand?" Molly protested. "I need the money. Besides, sometimes I think I'm making a big deal out of nothing. What if all he really *is* doing is telling jokes and goofing around? How do I know? I've never had a job before.

"I've thought of telling him how much it upsets me, but I'm scared to do that. What if he believes I'm just leading him on? Or worse yet, gets mad and fires me?"

Molly reached out and took a sip of water from Jake's glass. "See, it's not like Mr. Walters has ever said, 'If you let me do this and don't complain, you can keep your job and all the tips, but if you don't . . .' Still, that's how I feel. If I want raises and more hours, I know I'd better keep him happy."

She sighed. "I wish I could just get used to this. That's what Etta has done." She pointed toward the hostess who had seated them. "She's been here forever."

"Has he tried the same things with her?" Darby asked.

"I don't know how she's put up with it if he has. She's been here for years. Already I dread walking through the door, seeing him standing there smiling at me like we have some little secret we're sharing. He gives me the creeps!"

"I wish I could fix that guy," Jake said longingly. "Too bad you couldn't go undercover like the police do and wear a microphone. Then, when he said something really crude, bam! We could come in and arrest him!"

"I'd like to see him have to explain himself in court," Josh muttered. "Maybe we could show it live like they do on those crime shows on national television. It would be splashed all over the news, and he'd have to leave town in utter humiliation."

"Fantasizing about what you'd *like* to do isn't going to help," Gary commented pragmatically. "Molly, have you talked to your parents?"

"Are you kidding? They want me to have this job! Besides, I'm a junior in high school. Shouldn't I be old enough to handle this?" Molly stared wistfully into space. "Sometimes I wish I could be a little girl and tell them to fix everything . . . but I'm not. Besides, I *want* to be an adult.

"Maybe Mr. Walters picks on me because he can tell how young and dumb I am. If I'd had some experience, maybe this wouldn't have happened."

"Don't blame yourself. You aren't the cause of this problem."

"I'm not so sure my parents would agree. What if they blame me? What if they believe Mr. Walters' story and not mine? What if they won't let me work anymore or make huge trouble for the restaurant?" She dropped her head into her hands and groaned. "What if I just go crazy?"

"You can't let this go on, Molly." Gary's tone was gentle but firm.

Tears welled in Molly's eyes as Gary continued. "You're feeling very alone right now, but believe me, *you aren't alone.* This has happened to others. You aren't the only victim.

"If I were you, I'd already be interviewing for another job. But, since you know you want to continue in this one, you're going to have to deal with this problem head on. Sad to say, Walters might be the *first* problem you've ever had, but I doubt he'll be the last."

"So what am I going to do?"

"Quit or put a stop to it—or both."

"But how?"

"Tell him 'no.' Tell him that you do not want to be touched improperly ever again. Also tell him that you never want to hear another dirty joke. Tell him you will report him."

"But he *owns* this restaurant! How can I report the *boss*?"

"The United States has something called the Equal Employment Opportunities Commission. If there is no personnel department or higher authority to which to report your problem, file a complaint with the nearest EEOC office."

"That's too hard."

"Have your parents help you. Molly, what he's doing is not only *wrong*, it's *illegal*! What's more, it's illegal for him to fire you for complaining about it."

"No." Molly sagged backward in the booth, emotionally exhausted. "I need this job. I can't risk being fired. I need the money." She scraped her fingers through the blond halo of her hair. "Who knows? Maybe I'm unintentionally leading him on."

"Yeah, right. Like any of us would believe that!" Jake growled. "Molly, nobody I know thinks of you as a flirt, not even in high school. Why would you start flirting with your boss?"

"Jake's right," Josh agreed. "Guys respect you. They know you wouldn't throw yourself away. Don't sell yourself short. Where's your self-esteem?"

"Gone. Walters stole it."

"That does it." Gary's fist met the table. "Molly, you have to tell your parents about this."

Molly's eyes filled with panic. "No. Haven't you been *listening*? I can't . . ."

"He's got to be reported. If he's pulling stunts like this with you, he's probably doing it to others as well. It's not a matter of *if* he's going to be caught, but *when*. You can't brush this under the table, Molly."

"My parents would just die if they knew! They might blame me!"

"You'll have to go to them or I will."

"Please don't say anything! I'll stay away from him. I know how to do that. Gary, you can't tell anyone. Promise me?"

"I won't make a promise like that." Gary's jaw was set, the look in his gray-green eyes grim. "The best I will do is to give you the opportunity to tell your parents yourself. It would be better if they heard this from you than from me.

"Give them a little credit, Molly. They love you. They don't want to see you hurt. Let them help you."

"I can't . . . I can't. . . ."

"If you can't, I will. It's up to you."

Darby and Josh stared at each other across the table as Molly wept.

CHAPTER 8

LIVE

FROM DRENTWOOD HIGH

"Molly, Darby, could you wait a minute?" Ms. Wright looked up from her work as the girls walked past her desk. "I'd like to talk to you."

"Sure." Darby sank into a chair. Molly reiuctantly followed. She had been avoiding Ms. Wright ever since her conversation with Gary.

Just as Ms. Wright closed her textbook, Gary cruised into the room, a battered leather backpack flung across one shoulder. "Am I late?"

"Oh, great," Molly groaned. "Now they're ganging up on me!"

Ms. Wright gave Molly a compassionate look. "Please don't feel that way, Molly. Gary told me what happened. I'd hoped that you would realize that we can't overlook this situation. I understand that Gary has given you an opportunity to tell your parents what's been happening to you at work. Have you done so yet?"

Molly's pretty face hardened. "I told him I couldn't. I told him why too. I need that job. Ms. Wright, my stepdad is a mechanic, and my mom cleans homes for other people. How could they afford to send me to college? They're sweet, hard-working people. How could I *do* that to them?"

"I don't think you understand the full impact of what's happened to you, Molly. You may be in danger. A man who would fondle you in public might do practically anything if he ever had you alone in an isolated spot."

"He's a dirty old man, not a rapist!"

"Can you be one hundred percent sure of that?"

"Of course I can . . ." Molly hesitated. "I think." Her face crumpled. "Why is he doing this to me? *Why?*"

"Sexual harassment isn't always about sex, Molly."

"Then what's it about?" Darby asked.

"Sometimes it's about power."

"I don't understand." Molly looked hurt, puzzled, and afraid.

"Mr. Walters may enjoy seeing exactly how much power he has over you, Molly. He may get his 'kicks,' if you will, by seeing just how far he can go. He may get his pleasure from frightening you. He may enjoy knowing that he controls you, that without him you won't get a paycheck and would have trouble going to college. It appears he *does* have great power over you, Molly."

Gary settled his backpack on the floor and took a chair near the girls. The look on his face was thoughtful. "It may be power, Rosie, but it could be other things too."

"Such as?"

"Walters could just be a dirty old man. He doesn't care about Molly as a person. I think he sees her as a pretty girl who wouldn't give him a second glance if he weren't her boss and she didn't have to work for him.

He's bought into the messages our society sends about youth and sexuality. I'd say he sees you as a 'prize,' Molly, not a person."

Molly shivered. "Even talking about this makes me feel dirty . . . like I need to take a shower."

"We know this isn't easy to talk about, but you need to be aware of these things. Maybe Walters is nothing more than a silly man who's bought into a system that applauds 'macho' behavior, and harassing you makes him feel 'big.' Or he may be a very sick man who could be dangerous. We don't take this lightly, and you shouldn't either."

"You're scaring me."

"I'm sorry, but maybe you *need* to be scared. Scared enough to tell your parents what's been going on."

"But I said—"

"You do it or we do it. We'd be irresponsible if we demanded any less." Ms. Wright looked pensive. "Frankly, Molly, I'd like to pick up the phone right now and talk to your mom and dad."

"Wait!" The panicked expression on Molly's face threatened to dissolve into tears. She buried her face in her hands. "Give me a minute. I have to think."

The room was silent. Darby resisted the temptation to shuffle her feet.

When Molly began to speak, her voice was distant and thoughtful. "I never considered that I might be in danger. I've always thought that Mr. Walters was all hands and big talk, but I never felt that he might try to hurt me. I guess you're right though—how do I know? If he's bold enough to touch me like that in a public place, who knows what he might try if he ever got me alone?

"No one at work likes Mr. Walters—he's probably tried funny stuff with all of us. I suppose no one dares to say much because they are afraid of losing their jobs."

Molly ran her fingers through her blond curls. "I feel so *stupid*! I should know how to handle this!"

"Why do you say that?" Gary asked. "Where would a teenager learn to handle employers who sexually harass their employees?"

"Don't take the blame for this, Molly. It's not your fault."

"The fact that this situation developed is completely out of your control. What *is* in your control, however, is the decision to tell your parents."

"It's going to kill them. They probably won't even believe me! They think Walters is great because of his generous wage policy." A shadow slipped across Molly's features. "What if they make things even worse? What if they talk to Walters and he gets mad and punishes *me*? What's going to happen to me then?"

Gary and Ms. Wright exchanged a thoughtful glance. "Ideally, Molly? I'd like to see you get some counseling."

"*Me?* I'm not the crazy one!"

"Of course you aren't. You're the *victim*. Counseling would help you to understand what has happened to you and why. It would be a resource, providing ways for you to get through this."

"Get through what? He didn't rape me or anything. How do you know it's not all just teasing? So what if Mr. Walters is a jerk who thinks this sort of thing is funny? So what?"

A sob squeezed from Molly's throat. "*So what? So

he makes me feel like junk, that's what. And I hate it. I hate him!"

"We'll drive you home, Molly," Gary offered. "Rosie, Darby, and I will all come if you'd like. You don't have to talk to your parents alone."

Molly's eyes were glazed with tears, but her expression was determined. "No. I'll do it." She stood up and gathered her books to her chest. "And I'd better do it right now, before I lose my courage."

The room was silent as Molly walked, head held high, to the door.

CHAPTER 9

LIVE

FROM BRENTWOOD HIGH

Josh sauntered into the media room and flung his leather jacket onto an empty spot on the long worktable. Chaos Central had become the unofficial hangout of the *Live!* staff. When the students weren't working there, they were often studying on the large, disreputable couch in the "green room," a cubbyhole-like storage room that had been turned into a waiting room and lounge.

"Wait till you hear my idea!" he blurted.

Jake and Darby looked up from the wooden frames they were covering with canvas to be used as walls behind the news desk. The flats, which simulated walls, would be interchanged with other sets so as to make it look as though they were using more than one studio for taping.

"It must be good," Jake commented.

"It had *better* be good," Shane growled. "I can't concentrate with everybody talking." Shane was also working on scenic elements for the set. At the moment, he was preparing a mock window to hang behind the news desk.

"I passed the teachers' lounge on my way down the hall."

"No wonder you're excited," Julie said sarcastically. "I can hardly control myself when I see a room full of teachers."

Josh gave her a dirty look and continued. "It occurred to me that we're missing a valuable resource by not interviewing teachers as well as students on the topic of sexual harassment."

"What do *they* know?" Julie asked. Then a blush spread up her neck and across her cheeks. "Sorry, Ms. Wright. I guess I don't think of you as a teacher."

"Thank you . . . I think." Ms. Wright looked amused. She turned to Josh. "That's a great idea. Teachers are 'in the trenches,' so to speak. They deal with harassment on a regular basis."

"Do they? Then how come we never hear about it?"

"To respect a student's privacy." Ms. Wright grew pensive. "Teachers have an obligation to report problems such as these, you know."

"Really? You mean *you* could get into trouble if you didn't report something you saw or knew?"

"Something like that."

Across the room, Molly never lifted her eyes from the pages of her book. A pink flush bled up her neck.

"So even if a student didn't *want* you to report abuse, you'd *have* to?" Josh asked.

"Yes."

"I think it's a great idea, Josh." Darby opened her notebook to a fresh page. "Which teachers should we ask?"

"Why not ask *all* of them?"

"It's an hour show, Jake. We'd have to tape a whole month's worth of interviews if we talked to all the teachers!"

"It's up to you, but if *I* were working on this piece, I'd want as many interviews as I could get. How else will you know who has the most powerful story?"

Darby turned to Ms. Wright. "What do you think?"

"This is a learning experience. Seasoned production people know what they're looking for. This may help you to focus, to sift out the important facts from the less important ones. Do what you think you need to do."

"In other words," Josh rephrased, "it's up to us."

"Sounds like a lot of work to me," Kate grumbled.

"There's an *A* in it for you, Katie."

Kate gave Shane a dirty look. Before she could retort, however, Josh cleared his throat. "I say we go for it. My dad can give me some ideas as to which school principals I should call. They can tell us which teachers in the area might talk to us. We can take turns in the teachers' lounge here asking for volunteers. What do you think of that idea, Ms. Wright?"

A smile tugged at the corners of her lips. "I think, Joshua, that the teachers haven't got a chance against a persistent team like yours."

The conversation might have continued in that vein if Izzy had not appeared in the doorway just then with an odd expression on his face.

"Hi, Izz-man, whatcha up to . . ." Jake's voice trailed away. "What is *that*?"

All eyes turned toward Izzy's exposed forearm. From elbow to wrist a writhing red and blue snake twitched and wriggled on Izzy's skin.

"You *didn't*!"

"Izz, are you crazy?"

"A tattoo? Oh, Izzy . . ."

Sarah didn't say a word, but her eyes, wide and horrified, spoke volumes.

Even Ms. Wright registered a shocked expression. Only Gary, who as usual was a man of few words, grinned.

"What do you think?" Izzy flexed the muscles in his forearm and the snake squirmed. The little red tongue almost seemed to dart in and out.

"I think I'm going to puke," Julie announced. "Isador Eugene Mooney, you gross me out! You have absolutely gone too far with this research thing this time!"

"Oh, chill, Julie. It's not real."

There was a collective sigh of relief in the room. Ms. Wright rolled her eyes. Only Gary seemed unsurprised. Izzy focused his gaze on him. "You knew, didn't you?"

"I've seen a lot of tattoos in my time. It's a pretty good fake, though."

"If I don't wash my arm, it should stay on indefinitely."

"So you're going to become part of the great unwashed? Remind me not to sit next to you in class, Izzy."

"Just my arm." Izzy peered at the snake's tail near his wrist. "I took a bath this morning and I think I smeared this end a little. Does it ruin the effect?"

"Not a bit. But why did you do it?" Darby wondered. Now that she knew it was a fake, the ugly thing was a little easier to see.

"I've really been intrigued by my research at the tattoo shop. Did you know that tattoo artists practice their designs on grapefruits before they do their art on real people?"

"They must get sick of eating grapefruit," Kate muttered sarcastically. "And who says it's 'art' anyway?"

"That's what tattooing is, Kate—drawing or painting designs. The artist uses a needle instead of a brush and skin instead of canvas, that's all. Tattooing isn't easy, you know. The fellow I've been talking to even has tattoos inside his eyelids and lips—little stars, mostly. He does all his work freehand."

"I'm going to gag!" Kate yelped. "Stars inside his eyelids? He must be nuts! *You* must be nuts!"

"Doesn't that *hurt*?" Josh wondered.

"Burt—that's the tattoo artist's name—says it doesn't. Not very much, at least. The tattoo machine has a bunch of little needles on a bar. The needles vibrate up and down and don't penetrate very deeply. He says it's a weird feeling but not painful—just a sting."

"He'd have to say that. How else would he convince someone to get a tattoo anyway?"

"You'd never get me to do it," Jake said. "They're *permanent*."

"You mean you can never take off a tattoo?"

"Not without leaving a scar," Izzy admitted. "That's why no one should ever get a tattoo on a dare or without thinking it through first."

"Disgusting!" Kate shivered. "I hate this conversation."

"Izzy, you don't really mean to get a tattoo, do you?" Sarah's voice was soft and concerned.

"I don't know. Maybe. I just know that I think it's neat."

" 'You shall not make any gashes in your flesh for the dead or tattoo any marks upon you.' "

"Huh?"

"Leviticus 19:28. That's what it says in the Bible about tattoos."

Izzy looked intrigued. "You mean the *Bible* even talks about tattoos?"

"It talks about practically everything," Sarah answered with a smile. "All you have to do is look."

"Hmmmm." Izzy appeared thoughtful. "I didn't know God had an opinion about tattoos."

"Tattoos used to be used to identify criminals and slaves in ancient Greece and Rome," Gary commented.

"I always knew Izzy had criminal tendencies," Julie said. "This proves it."

"Maybe I need to think about this some more," Izzy concluded. "But, I still like my snake." He twitched the muscles in his arm, and Julie groaned. "And the reaction it brings."

"I hate to break up this intellectual conversation," Jake said, "but Darby and I are going out for fries and a shake. Anyone interested in coming along?" Jake put his hand on Darby's shoulder, and she smiled up at him.

"Food? Why didn't you say so earlier?" Izzy lunged for the door, his tattoo forgotten. "I haven't eaten anything since lunch, except for a few candy bars and an old sandwich I found in my locker. Let's go!"

———

"Kate, you're running camera one."

Kate grimaced at Gary's instruction.

"I know you want to be in front of the camera, but it's important that all of you take a turn at the technical side of this."

Competition for the anchor spots on *Live!* was

fierce. The only ones who didn't seem to mind being behind the scenes were Sarah, Izzy, and Shane. Izzy was totally absorbed with the technical side of things, and Shane kept aloof from the entire process. Sarah rarely complained about anything.

"You have to remember, Kate, that the jobs behind the camera are equal to or more important than the 'glory' jobs on camera. The 'talent' wouldn't even get on the air if it weren't for the director, the camera people, the—"

"I still think the important thing is to be an interviewer." Julie took up Kate's cause. "No one sees the others. And that's what it's all about, isn't it? Being seen?"

"I don't want to hear any more of this unprofessional whining while you are supposed to be working." Gary scowled. "If some of you don't have an attitude turnaround pretty soon, you aren't going to last in this program."

Julie clamped her lips together and frowned. Gary didn't speak often, but when he did, everyone knew enough to listen.

"Molly is going to have all the fun," Kate muttered as she reluctantly took her place behind the camera and began to ready herself for taping.

"Yeah, right. Molly's going to have fun." Josh looked at Darby. "Do you think she'll get through this without breaking down?"

"She said she'd wanted to do the teacher interviews. I tried to talk her out of it, but she insisted. She must think she can manage it."

"Molly is looking for answers," Josh deduced. "I

know I would be if I were in her shoes. Maybe this will be good for her."

"At least she's figured out that she's not alone with her problem," Darby added. "Everywhere we turn lately, we hear another story about sexual harassment. I never dreamed it was so common."

"Have either of you looked into the green room?" Jake asked as he came up beside them. "It's the funniest thing I've ever seen!"

"What?"

"Shane Donahue trying to relax a bunch of nervous teachers!"

"Shane?" Josh and Darby burst into laughter. Shane's surly bad-boy image was well known. The idea of him trying to comfort a teacher was truly bizarre. No wonder they were nervous!

At that moment Shane ushered the first of the teacher interviewees into the studio. Taping was about to begin.

"Do you agree with the statement made by our last guest that sexual harassment often begins in schools?" Molly looked cool and poised as she voiced her questions for the camera. Darby and Josh, however, could see her hands trembling and the delicate beads of perspiration gathering at her temples.

"Is it that hot under the lights, or is that nerves?" Josh whispered.

"Both, I think. She's doing all right, though, isn't she?"

"Better than I expected. Maybe she's finally coming around and admitting to herself what a problem this is."

"Shhhh!" Kate hissed. "I want to hear this!"

"Unfortunately, that statement may be correct." Mrs. Tamara Williams, an elementary schoolteacher from Harbor Elementary appeared troubled. "For many children, school is their first opportunity to spend a great deal of time with children of the opposite sex. It is a time in which they must learn what is or isn't acceptable behavior.

"According to reports I've received, nearly eighty percent of all teenagers report being sexually harassed in some way or another—by comments, jokes, touches, stares. Even boys are harassed—usually by comments or notes sent by girls. Still, it seems girls more regularly experience harassment."

"How would you define sexual harassment?"

Mrs. Williams thought for a moment. "Any sort of inappropriate and unwelcome sexual behavior." Her eyes clouded. "It is a very difficult situation for students. Fear, intimidation, and inexperience play big roles in harassment."

"You sound as though you know from personal experience."

Ms. Wright glanced up sharply at Molly's comment. She had strayed from the planned interview.

"I do. I was. In college, the head of my major's department offered me good grades if I would go out with him. He also threatened that I might 'flunk' if I didn't fulfill his wishes."

"Really?" Molly's eyes grew round, the script forgotten. "What did you do?"

"For a long time I did nothing. Then, when I finally got enough courage, I reported him to the administration."

"What happened? Did you get in trouble?"

"No, but *he* did. He was asked to leave the school. It was a terrifying time for me, but I'm glad I was brave enough to do the right thing."

"Do you have any regrets?"

"None, except that I wish I'd reported him earlier and saved myself a lot of grief. The good thing that came out of all this is the fact that I feel that I can truly understand a child who is experiencing something similar."

"What do you suggest schools should do about sexual harassment?"

"Take active steps to prevent it or to stop it if it is already happening. A child cannot learn if school is not a safe place for him or her to be. Students deserve an environment that's safe and conducive to learning. Teachers and administrators have an obligation to provide that or risk censure.

"The only way to put a stop to harassment is to face it head on. Children should be encouraged to say 'no' to anyone who engages in unacceptable behavior. We have to stop more children from being victims—even victims of their own peers.

"You've heard of just saying 'no' to drugs. Kids have to learn to say 'no' to harassment as well."

"Why do you think so little is said or done about sexual harassment in schools?"

"Good question," Ms. Wright whispered to no one in particular.

"Partly because of the idea that this behavior is 'play' of some sort," Mrs. Williams continued. "That it is funny and harmless. But it isn't harmless—not when it hurts children mentally and emotionally. It's time we begin to set limits and demand sexual restraint of our young people."

———

"Wait up!"

Darby and Molly turned around at the sound of the familiar voice. Josh loped toward them, dodging mall benches and planters filled with artificial ficus trees.

"I've been chasing you ever since you came out of

Music World," he panted. "Do you take vitamins before you go shopping or what?"

"Serious shopping allows no time for goofing off," Darby said with a laugh. "We power walk!"

"I need a 'power' rest. Want a soda?"

"Sure. I could use a break." Molly led the way into the food court. "In fact, I'll buy."

When Molly returned with the beverages in hand, she stopped in front of Josh. "What are you staring at?"

"Nothing, really." He looked embarrassed. "It's just that now that I've got you here, I don't know how to start."

"Start what?" Molly's eyes narrowed suspiciously.

Josh took a deep breath and plunged. "I wanted to tell you how much I admire you."

Molly's eyes widened in surprise. "Me?" The word came out in a squeak.

"I've been watching you, and I know how hard doing this story has been for you." Josh's eyes clouded. "I know I can't understand your problem exactly, but I *do* know what it's like not to be respected and that it's hard not to slink into a corner and blame yourself for what's going wrong. Don't ever forget that it is Mr. Walters who is in the wrong, not you!"

"That's really sweet of you, Josh." Tears welled in Molly's eyes. "I needed to hear that today."

"Trouble?" Darby asked softly.

"I don't know. I did what Gary and Ms. Wright said I had to do. I told my folks. They were pretty bummed by it all. I don't know what's going to happen now."

She scrubbed at her eyes. "I feel so dirty and so weak."

Josh's eyes flashed. "Don't! Listen, if I were to believe the people who look down on me because I'm black, I'd be a real mess. You can't let anyone treat you as a second-class citizen just because you are a female any more than I should allow myself to be walked all over because I was born black not white! Sure it's de-humanizing and hard on the self-esteem, but you have to keep reminding yourself that *you are a good person*."

"No matter what other people say or do, you are still in control of your life," Darby added.

"Yeah, right. I sure am. At this minute I feel totally *out* of control!"

"You're the one who calls the next step. Do you let Walters continue with his sick little game, or do you put a stop to it? It seems to me that by telling your parents, you *have* taken control of the situation."

"Maybe you're right," Molly murmured. "For a long time I thought that there was nothing I could do. Now, at least, I'm beginning to realize that I can choose how to react."

"And how to affect your entire life."

Josh slurped thoughtfully on his soda for a moment. "Think good thoughts about yourself, Molly. Don't buy into the 'I'm bad because this is happening to me' thing. Don't let Walters take away your self-esteem."

They were all concentrating so hard that no one heard Sarah roll her wheelchair up beside them. "Am I interrupting?"

Darby jumped and Molly gave a little squeak.

"If you want me to leave . . ."

"No. Stay. You're good at serious conversations, Sarah. We need you." Molly blurted out what they had been discussing.

Sarah nodded sagely, her brown eyes wise. "I've been thinking a lot about you lately, Molly. And praying too. I hope you don't mind."

"I need all the help I can get. Does the Bible say anything about sexual harassment? You always tell us it has something to say about everything."

Sarah smiled and, as always, her eyes lit with a tranquil glow that came from deep within her. "Lately I've been reading about Esau and Jacob."

"Who are they?"

"The twin sons of Isaac of the Bible."

"I should have known."

"In those days a 'birthright' was given to the first son born to a family," Sarah explained. "That meant the first son would receive a double share of the family's inheritance and someday become the leader of the family. Esau, because he was hungry, traded his birthright away to his brother Jacob in exchange for some food. Jacob tricked Esau into giving away something personal and of great value."

"Big dummy! Even I'd know better than to do that!" Molly said. "So what do Esau and Jacob have to do with me?"

"Women have traditionally accepted their role in a male-run society. Now they are beginning to wonder if they've somehow lost or been tricked out of their right to be equal human beings, on the same level as men. Just like Jacob tricked Esau out of his birthright, some men try to steal women's right to respect and equality. Your boss is one of those men."

"Only you would think like that, Sarah!" Molly blurted. "I wish I knew the Bible like you did. Maybe then I could figure some of this out."

"You can," Sarah pointed out. "Here." She put a book into Molly's hands. "Take this. I have another at home."

Molly stared at the Bible suspiciously. Sarah chuckled. "Try it; you might like it. Even if it doesn't mention Mr. Walters by name, the Bible does talk a lot about self-respect and forgiveness. It can't hurt."

Tears began to stream down Molly's cheeks.

"I didn't mean to upset you . . ." Sarah looked alarmed.

"You'd just give this to me? I didn't know you cared!" Molly sniffled. "It's so weird . . . and wonderful . . . to know that I actually have friends who are concerned about what happens to me . . . who worry about me!"

Darby put her arms around Molly. Josh did the same. Sarah laid her hand on Molly's wrist.

"We're behind you one hundred percent," Josh said. "Whatever happens, we're with you."

Molly drooped visibly in their arms. "How did I ever get *into* this mess?" she moaned. "How?"

"You didn't go looking for this, Molly. It found you . . ."

". . . and now you'll have to do something about it."

"I know. I know." Molly put back her head, and tears streamed down her face and onto the collar of her shirt. "But why is it so hard?"

"Who wants to come with me?" Josh dangled car keys in Jake's face. "I'm going to the video store at the mall to return these tapes my dad rented yesterday."

"Can't. I've got three tests tomorrow." Jake leaned

heavily against the ratty couch cushion in the green room. "I've got to go home."

"Did I hear someone say 'mall'?" Darby inquired. "I promised I'd pick up a jacket for my mom after school. If I rode over with you, it would save a lot of time. Do you mind if I go along?"

Josh nodded. "Then let's go."

"Should we drop the tapes off first?" At Darby's nod, Josh pulled into the parking lot.

Darby and Josh walked into the empty store. A heavyset man with dark hair and a sour expression hovered behind the desk.

"I'm here to return these tapes for Harold Willis," Josh began hesitantly.

The man scowled at them fiercely. "Are they late?"

"N-no. At least I don't *think* so. My dad just asked me to return them this morning."

"You kids. Nothing but trouble. Always trying to say things aren't late and they are. Don't know what's happened to young people today. Can't tell the truth for anything." He punched up Mr. Willis's name on his computer. "Don't know where this country is going but I don't like it . . . oh, here you are." He had the grace to look embarrassed. "Right on time."

Darby cast a covert glance at Josh. His mouth was working furiously and his eyes glittered. She'd never seen him so angry.

"Sir," he began. "I'm sorry you've had bad experiences with teenagers, but we aren't *all* dishonest or disrespectful."

"Maybe not, but I don't have much proof of that." Josh's comment seemed to have tapped a well about to overflow. "Kids nowadays are spoiled rotten and like to cause trouble." He picked up a letter that lay next to the cash register. "Like this! Kids like you are trying to ruin my life!"

Darby tugged on Josh's sleeve, eager to leave, but Josh ignored her. "Sir?"

"Do you know what this is?" the man demanded. "A letter from a lawyer! He says that he's had a complaint from my employees. Says I'm providing an 'inappropriate' work environment for my female employees! Says they're crying 'sexual harassment' at work!"

Darby's eyes grew round, and Josh's expression turned cunning. Neither spoke.

"What is 'sexual harassment' anyway? The girls come in here dressed in miniskirts and tight blouses and then don't want anyone to notice? Hah! They want *everybody* to notice—they just don't want anyone to do anything about it. Girls wear sweaters three sizes too small and then whine and cry when someone accidently brushes up against them. What are the men who work here supposed to do anyway? Put blinders on?

"This complaint could ruin me! What a filthy, rotten trick! If they don't want to be noticed, why do they dress that way?"

Suddenly the man's expression grew cautious. "But I don't need to tell you this. You kids couldn't understand. You have no idea what it's like to find yourself ruined ... ruined. ..."

The man turned away from them, his shoulders sagging. It was as though Darby and Josh weren't even there.

They escaped to the car. Darby's knees were knocking, and Josh's hand trembled as he attempted to unlock the door. Once inside the car, Darby sagged against the seat and closed her eyes. "We really walked into something there!"

"That letter must have arrived just minutes before we got to the store," Josh deduced. "I've never seen anyone behave like that! He was in a blind rage. I wished we'd never come."

Darby chewed at the corner of her lip thoughtfully. "I don't. Josh, this is an angle we hadn't even considered. We've assumed that everyone who says they've been sexually harassed was telling the truth. It is possible that people could lie about such a thing. Maybe that man's employees didn't like him. He certainly is a jerk. Maybe it *was* a vicious trick."

"And maybe not." Josh closed his eyes.

"Ms. Wright said it was important that we keep an 'open mind' about everything we learned and that we tell both sides of every story."

"I don't like to think that a guy like that might actually be right," Josh admitted, "but I suppose it could happen."

"At the beginning of the program, Ms. Wright promised us that we'd learn to 'think' and to 'question,'" Darby murmured. "I've been 'thinking' and 'questioning' until my head hurts!"

It wasn't until Josh had dropped her off at her front door that Darby realized that she'd completely forgotten to pick up her mother's jacket at the mall.

"We need an inky-dinky over here!" Izzy yelled. Every head in the studio lifted except Gary's.

"What's an 'inky-dinky'?" Julie asked. "Or did you just make that up, Izzy?"

Izzy looked insulted as Jake and Sarah, who were seated behind the news desk on the set, burst into laughter.

"An 'inky-dinky' is another name for a baby spot-light," Gary offered. "It is mounted on the camera and controlled by the camera operator with a dimmer. It is used to adjust the lighting when the key light can't be brought close enough to the subject being filmed. In this case, that's Sarah and Jake. I see Izzy has been reading his textbook."

"Yeah, Julie. What'd you *think* I was referring to when I said 'inky-dinky'? Your brain?"

"That's enough, you two," Gary sighed. "You're giving me a headache."

"I'm getting a headache looking at that ugly thing on his arm," Julie snapped. "Aren't you ever going to get rid of that horrible fake tattoo?"

Izzy flexed his muscle in Julie's face. The snake twitched and Julie shuddered. "You're disgusting!"

"I talked to the tattoo artist again," Izzy announced. "He's really awesome. I like a guy who tries to make a statement."

"What's your statement, Izzy? That you're nuts?"

"Izzy, don't be taken in by the guy. He's just out to make a buck. How much does he charge to make a 'statement' on your skin?"

Izzy shook his head. "I'm not telling. If you want to know the whole story, read my in-depth article when it comes out."

"Izzy, you aren't thinking of actually *getting* a tattoo, are you?" Sarah looked askance.

"Ah, Sarah, it's no big deal. Just a few needle pricks and a little paint, that's all. What's one little tattoo on a body that has as much skin as mine?" Izzy was trying hard to sell himself on the idea of getting a tattoo.

"Izzy, you are the most squeamish guy I know. That you'd even *consider* letting someone poke you with a bunch of needles is beyond me."

"I could do it. I know I could. It's not like watching a baby be born or—ow! What'd you do that for, Sarah?"

Sarah, who had been listening quietly, rolled her wheelchair over Izzy's feet and bumped him in the shins with her chair.

"Just trying to knock a little sense into you, that's all. Talk doesn't seem to do it, so I thought I'd try this."

"I've got plenty of sense!" he protested indignantly, rubbing his shin.

"Not if you get a tattoo, you don't."

"I don't see what the big deal is. It's my body, isn't it?"

"I'm serious, Izzy. You may get a tattoo now to make a 'statement' of some sort, but what if, in fifteen or twenty years, that statement isn't true for you any-more? What if that tattoo is no longer what you rep-resent? You said yourself that a tattoo is a permanent decision."

"It's not like it's etched in marble. They can be sur-gically removed."

"Surgery involves needles, knives, blood, and scars, doesn't it?"

Izzy swallowed thickly. "So?"

"You're the guy who got sick thinking about getting a tetanus shot! How are you ever going to handle being punched by a million needle pricks in order to get that tattoo? Or, worse yet, the operation it would take to have it removed?"

Sarah reached out and put her hand over Izzy's. Her expression was intent. "Think about this, Izzy. Con-sider every angle before you do anything drastic. You don't need a tattoo to tell the world who you are." She smiled briefly. "Izz-man, you're a 'statement' already. Don't foolishly mark up your body. It's God's *temple*."

"Huh?"

"You are one of God's creations, Izzy—His 'temple.' I'm not sure it's good to write graffiti all over the walls of one of His living temples."

"I sure don't feel much like a temple."

"None of us do, but that doesn't change the fact that we are. At least promise me that you'll think hard be-fore you do anything foolish. Please?"

"Give me a break, Sarah! This is for *fun*. Everybody can use a little gimmick, something unique to make him stand out in a crowd."

"I don't buy that Izzy. You don't need a 'gimmick.' You've already been created by God in His own image.

What better 'gimmick' is there than that? You're meant to be just the way you are. Surely you can't be any better than that!"

"Oww, Sarah, you know I never know what to say when you start talking that 'God' stuff."

"Then don't say anything. Just promise me you'll think about what I said."

"Sarah, I'd do anything for you. You know that. I promise. But I *still* don't see what the big fuss is about. . . ."

Gary cleared his throat. "Excuse me, but would anyone mind if I butted into this conversation?"

"Jump right in," Izzy invited. "We're not getting very far anyway."

Now the attention of the entire room was focused on Izzy, Sarah, and Gary. Everyone liked to hear Gary talk. Whatever he said was always smart, savvy, relevant—and rarely preachy.

Solemnly, he rolled up the shirt sleeve on his left arm. Julie gasped. Everyone stared. There, on his forearm, was a tattoo of an ornate dagger, with his name inscribed on the hilt. A single drop of red blood dripped dramatically off the tip of the blade.

"Neat!" Izzy exclaimed. "I didn't know you had that. Why didn't you tell me?"

"Ewwww!" Kate wrinkled her nose. "It looks *mean*."

"You don't seem like the kind of guy who'd want a dagger on his arm."

Gary arched one eyebrow. "I've changed since this was done. It's true what Sarah says about making a statement. Sometimes you change as a person, and the tattoo can't change with you."

"When did you get it?"

"In the navy. A bunch of my buddies and I dared each other to do it. That, by the way, is a *lousy* reason to get a tattoo. But, being young and dumb, we all ended up with one."

"I think it's really cool." Izzy stared at Gary's arm in open admiration.

"I used to think the same way, but not anymore."

"Why a dagger?"

"Because it looked tough. And because I liked that little drop of blood just off the tip. I thought it would make guys think twice before picking a fight with me."

"Did it work?"

"Maybe later. At first I couldn't have been in a fight even if I'd wanted to."

"What do you mean?"

"Any pride or pleasure I might have received from this dagger was outweighed by the trouble it caused. You see, as a result of unclean tattooing equipment, I came down with a raging case of hepatitis."

Izzy blanched. For all his bravado about getting a tattoo, he still hadn't overcome his innate squeamishness.

"I didn't even think about health hazards," Gary continued. "It seemed so easy at the time. The guy who did it seemed to know his stuff. He even had little temporary tattoos he used as an outline to follow. That way we could see what we were getting before we actually did it.

"It didn't really hurt once he got the outline done. Filling in the color was no big deal. When it was over, I assumed it was over for good. That is, of course, until I got sick."

"Sick?"

"I thought it was a bug of some sort—mononucleosis, maybe. I ran a temperature and ached all over. When I ended up in the infirmary, they ran some liver tests and discovered it was hepatitis. Three of my buddies had it too."

"Are you sure it was from the tattoo?"

"Positive. I hadn't engaged in any other risky behavior. Hepatitis can be transferred from one person to another in the same ways the AIDS virus is transferred. You can also get it from eating bad food, but I'd been eating navy food with a hundred other guys, and they didn't get sick."

"Bummer."

"Actually, I was lucky. I didn't get the *chronic* form of the disease—or, worse yet, AIDS. I was young and dumb, Izzy. Thanks to that tattoo, I could have ended up dead. I know this isn't what you want to hear, but I agree with Sarah. Don't mess with your body. Respect it. Take care of it."

Izzy's normally pale complexion had taken on a greenish cast. Everyone in the room had moved to surround him and Gary, fascinated by the conversation.

"Getting a tattoo was one of the dumbest things I've ever done." Gary grinned. "And I've done a few."

"I never thought . . ." Izzy's voice trailed away. His shoulders drooped.

Suddenly he punched a fist into the palm of his other hand. "I blew it!"

"Why do you say that? You haven't got a real tattoo yet . . ." Sarah's voice trembled, "*have* you?"

"No. But I must be a really crummy investigative reporter," Izzy lamented. "I didn't even *think* about looking at the 'downside' or the health risks of getting a tattoo. I didn't cover all the angles. I would have written a one-sided, slanted piece that wouldn't have shown the entire picture."

"Don't be too hard on yourself," Gary said. "After all, the story isn't written yet. Consider our conversation today 'research.' Besides, investigative reporting takes practice. You've learned something, haven't you?"

Izzy nodded.

"That's what counts—especially if you're considering a tattoo. All I ask is that you not learn the hard way if you can learn from me."

Izzy abruptly stood up. "I've got to go. I need to talk to that guy at the tattoo parlor."

As he strode out of the room, Julie sighed. "Well, I hope that little episode is over!"

Everyone in the room was in full agreement.

"Are you going to the studio?" Sarah asked as she and Darby moved down the hall.

"In a minute. I have to wash my hands first. I've still got paint on them from art class. See you there." Humming, Darby turned into the rest room. A slender girl with pale brown hair was standing over the sink, her eyes averted.

"Hi," Darby said. She put her books on the ledge over the sink and turned on the water faucet. Over the sound of rushing water, Darby heard another noise. Crying.

The girl next to her had turned toward the wall.

Her shoulders were trembling and ragged sobs were choking from her.

"Are you okay?"

"Go away."

"If there's anything I can do . . ."

"There's nothing anybody can do. Go away."

It took a moment for Darby to recognize Gerilyn McDonald. Then the puzzle pieces began to fit into place.

"I don't think you know me, Gerilyn," Darby began, "but I know who you are and—"

"Everybody knows me! All the guys at least." Gerilyn turned around. Her eyes were wet and swollen with tears. "Isn't that great? Isn't that what every girl wants?"

"I know about the graffiti in the locker room, and I think it's terrible," Darby said.

"Terrible? Aren't you *envious*? Every guy at Brentwood has my telephone number." It was horrible seeing Gerilyn try to joke away the pain.

"You don't have to pretend with me," Darby said softly. "I'm on the *Live! From Brentwood High* staff. We're doing a piece on sexual harassment. I know how awful it is."

Gerilyn stared at her. "How could you know if it hasn't happened to you? How could you know how humiliating it is to hear the filthy stuff that's written about you and have no way to stop it? I'm not allowed in the locker room or I'd get rid of it myself. My parents tried to talk to someone here at the school, and he just put down the whole thing—said we'd make it worse if we made a big deal of it. So now what do I do? Pretend I don't know? Pretend I don't *care*?"

Someone cleared their throat in the doorway. Gerilyn and Darby looked up to see Ms. Wright standing there, her arms crossed over her chest, her face a mask of outrage.

Gerilyn clamped a hand over her mouth. "Oh no!"

Ms. Wright moved into the room. "Is this true?"

Darby nodded numbly. "All the guys know about it. We girls just started hearing about it recently. I don't know why they picked on Gerilyn. Maybe because she's shy and they thought it was funny."

"Funny?" Ms. Wright shook her head. "How have we let it come to this?"

"What do you mean?"

"There is a fine line between flirting and harassment, between humor and cruelty. Obviously we haven't taught our students the difference." Ms. Wright put an arm around Gerilyn's shoulder.

"I don't know who your parents talked to, but they didn't talk to *me*. I promise you this—this harassment will stop—even if it means I have to remove the doors in the boys' locker room myself! Come with me."

Darby watched Gerilyn and Ms. Wright leave the room. Then she breathed a sigh of relief, confident that, finally, something would be done.

CHAPTER 12

LIVE

FROM BRENTWOOD HIGH

"Molly? It's Darby. What are you doing?" Darby held the telephone receiver between her ear and her shoulder as she spoke.

"Not much. Mom made me clean my room today. I'm just finishing my laundry."

"Can you come over to my place?"

"What's up?"

"Jake just called. He and his sister are coming over. His sister would like to meet you."

"Me? Why?"

"Can you come or can't you?"

"I suppose, but I don't understand . . ."

"Hurry. They'll be here soon." Darby hung up the phone.

———

When Molly arrived, she wore a puzzled expression. "What was all that mystery about on the phone? Why does Jake's sister want to meet me? What's going on—"

"Here they come!" Darby interrupted Molly's questions to greet Jake and his sister at the door.

"Hi, Darby, Molly. This is my sister Kathy."

"Hello. I'm so glad to meet you!" Kathy had sandy-blond hair and gray-green eyes just like Jake's, and her smile was equally wide and attractive. It was obvious by the way Jake held open the door and escorted his sister to a seat in the living room that he was very fond of her.

"We've heard a lot about you," Darby began.

Laughter bubbled from Kathy. "I'm sure you have. Jake takes every opportunity to tell people that his sisters practically 'ruined' him."

"Not exactly . . ."

"I'll admit it. From the day he was born, we thought he was our own little toy. But he turned out all right anyway, don't you think?" Kathy's eyes twinkled. "A bit of a hunk, in fact."

"Kathy!" Jake growled as a blush crept up his neck and across his cheeks.

"Are you Jake's youngest sister?" Molly wondered, still puzzled as to why she—and they—were here.

"No. I'm in the middle of the pack. We're all very close in age. In fact, sometimes Dad would just call us One, Two, Three, and Four. I'm Two."

Kathy looked around the living room. "Nice house. Jake says my dad built it."

"Isn't that a great coincidence? My dad was so surprised. . . ."

Molly was getting restless with the small talk. She shifted in her chair and scowled at Darby. Finally she blurted, "*Why* are we here? I don't mean to be rude or anything, but this seems very strange. . . ."

Kathy and Darby grew very still. Jake cleared his throat a number of times before speaking.

"Molly, I asked my sister if she'd be willing to talk

to you. She has a story that might be of interest to you."

Molly's expression grew guarded. "What kind of story?"

"Come, sit next to me." Kathy patted the couch cushion next to her.

Warily Molly approached. "What's going on?"

"Please don't be angry with Jake, but he told me what has happened to you at work."

"Jake! You shouldn't have!" Molly flushed furiously.

"Don't worry. It won't go any further. Jake only told me because I've had a similar experience. He thought it might help you if we could talk."

"Similar?" Molly said doubtfully. "I don't think . . ."

"I was sexually harassed by a professor when I was in college."

Molly grew still as Kathy continued.

"I was barely eighteen, young for a college freshman, and had had very few dating experiences. My professor was one of the most popular on campus. His classes always filled up early. He devoted a lot of time to his students and often invited them to his apartment for study sessions. For a girl who was feeling lost in the college system, that seemed pretty awesome. Immediately, I was as devoted to him as the rest of his students."

Kathy's pretty face took on a haunted look. "One night after study group, he asked me to stay behind and go over some questions I was struggling with. It seemed generous of him to want to help me, so I stayed. Then he tried to rape me."

A soft groan escaped Molly's lips.

"I got away and ran home crying. My roommate was

already asleep, so I tiptoed into the shower and stood there for nearly an hour—trying to wash away his fingerprints on my skin. I'd never felt so dirty, so violated.

"After that, I sank into a terrible depression. I dropped his class and never told anyone why. Finally, my parents insisted I see a counselor. That's when I told them what happened."

"What did they do?"

"They went to the administration of the college and reported what had happened."

"Then what?" Kathy had Molly's full attention.

"At first, they didn't want to believe it was possible. As I said, he was a very popular professor. Still, after an investigation it was discovered that I wasn't the first or only girl he'd tried to seduce. Others had had the same experience and been afraid to come forward. One girl thought she wouldn't be believed; another didn't want to be involved in the publicity she was afraid might occur if the news media got ahold of the story. Another committed suicide."

"Oh!" Molly covered her face with her hands.

"At first he tried to say that I'd consented to his advances prior to changing my mind. After a while, he tried to alter his story. Pretty soon he had himself tangled in a web of lies. Shortly thereafter he was asked to leave the college."

Kathy took Molly's hand. "Jake asked me to talk to you because he understands how frightening something like this can be. He remembers my tears and my pain. I suffered for a long time, Molly, afraid that I'd ruined a man's life. I worried that I'd brought this on myself until I finally realized that no matter what I'd done, my professor's behavior was not appropriate. He was the adult, the person in a position of authority. He abused that authority and tried to hurt me. No one should do that. My parents and I *had* to speak out. There were others to protect, girls as innocent and naive as I was. Someone *had* to speak out. Do you understand?"

"My parents said they'd deal with Mr. Walters," Molly murmured, "but I'm so *scared*. He's going to hate me. I'm not going to have a job. Maybe, because of him, I won't get to college...."

"Trust your parents. I wish I'd done that far sooner. Let them help you. I often think of the girl who committed suicide. If only she'd allowed someone to help her!"

"So you don't think I'm being a big baby about all of this?"

"No. Your body is your private property. No one has the right to touch it without your permission. Your boss went too far. He stepped over the line of propriety. He's the one who is wrong, not you."

Kathy touched a finger to Molly's cheek. "You have to take charge now. Don't let the world run you. Make choices. Make decisions that will benefit you. Power and control come from inside yourself. Don't hand the power to control your life over to a stranger."

"It's like knowing you are created by God and are good just the way you are, isn't it? My friend Sarah said something like that yesterday."

Kathy looked surprised. "That's a good way to put it. 'God-made and glad of it'—that's what my grandmother used to say."

"But it's still hard." Molly sighed.

"True. But it's doable. You can get through this. Besides, even the *law* is on your side. Your boss is engaging in illegal activity when he treats you as he does."

"I wish none of this had ever happened," Molly groaned.

"I know what you mean. For a while, I thought I'd never get over what happened to me, but time is a great healer. I don't think of it very often now, and when I do, I think of what I learned, of how it made me a stronger, braver person. Learn from this, Molly; don't be crushed by it!"

Unexpectedly Molly launched herself into Kathy's arms. They clung to each other, bound by the events that had touched them. Kathy stroked Molly's hair. "It will be okay. It will. Believe me."

After a while, Molly drew away and scrubbed at her eyes with her fists. "I didn't know how good it would feel to know I'm not alone."

"Misery loves company," Kathy said ruefully.

Jake's hand closed over Darby's as they sat quietly, totally involved yet so much apart from what was happening between Kathy and Molly. Tears streamed down Darby's face, but she made no move to wipe them away.

"Kathy, would you consider being a part of our television feature?" Molly asked. She flushed. "An hour ago, I wouldn't have dreamed of asking you this, but for the first time since this mess started, I've heard something that makes sense to me. Harassment is about power and about self-esteem. No woman should have to give up either. All along I've been worrying about money and my job. But all the money in the world can't make me feel happy with myself if I allow Walters to do this to me anymore!"

Molly's jaw firmed with resolve. "So what if I have to work two jobs to make enough for college? So what if I can't have all the new clothes I'd like? I can do it! I think I could do practically *anything* if I had Walters off my back!"

Kathy grinned through the sheen of tears in her eyes. "I convinced you of all that? Wow. I must be good."

Molly burst into genuine laughter. "You are. Everybody's been hammering the same thoughts at me, but just now, with you, it all seemed to click. Maybe, if you came on our show, you could do it for someone else too!"

"I don't know . . ." Kathy looked contemplative.

Jake squeezed Darby's hand, and they both held their breath, waiting for her answer.

"Oh, why not? If you thought it would help someone else, I could do it."

Kathy's expression grew grim. "When it comes right down to it, I guess I'd do just about *anything* to put an end to sexual harassment. It's demeaning, it's dehumanizing, and it's *wrong*. . . ."

Kathy put a hand over her mouth. "Maybe I should save my soapbox speech for television."

Jake stood up and moved toward his sister. "Thank you—for agreeing to be on the show—and for Molly."

Kathy hugged her brother and winked at Darby. "We Saunders girls raised our baby brother right. I hope the girls at Brentwood High appreciate that."

Darby blushed from head to toe as Kathy winked at her. Jake squirmed self-consciously.

"Well, if you don't have any more questions for me, I'd better go." Kathy dusted her hands together and grinned impishly. "Now that I've managed to embarrass both Darby and my brother, my job here is done. Jake, can you give me a ride to the clinic?"

"Clinic? Are you sick?" Molly's brow wrinkled in concern.

"Not at all. I volunteer at a free clinic on the north side. Today is immunization day, and it's going to be busy."

"A free clinic?" Darby mused. "What a great story idea!"

Kathy nodded enthusiastically. "You really should visit sometime. Doctors, nurses, staff, all donating their time and talent to people who wouldn't otherwise be able to afford health care. I'm surprised Jake didn't tell you about it before now."

"Let's mention it to Ms. Wright," Darby suggested. "What do you think, Molly?"

But Molly didn't answer. She was already lost in her own thoughts.

"Darby, phone's for you," Mrs. Ellison called from the kitchen.

"Who is it?"

"Answer and find out for yourself."

"Boy or girl?"

"Darby, just pick up the phone! Why do we go through this ritual every time the phone rings?"

Darby blushed. "I like to know in advance if it's Jake."

"Well, it's not Jake, but it's a male voice. Does that help?"

Nothing, however, could have prepared Darby for the voice on the other end of the line.

"Hi, this is Shane Donahue."

Darby nearly dropped the phone. There was a time when she'd have practically melted to hear Shane's voice on the other end of the line. Now, thanks to Jake, she was only surprised. "What's up?"

"Not much. Is your team done with the harassment story yet?"

Darby hadn't realized that Shane was paying attention to her team's project. Of course, he had suggested that they interview guys as well as girls about sexual harassment, and the idea had been a good one. Maybe Shane was more interested than anyone had given him credit for being.

"We're still working. It's become a much bigger story than we'd planned. Ms. Wright has given us more air time. She says we can have up to an hour if we need it. It's turning into a documentary!"

"Oh."

"Why do you ask?"

"Just wondering."

Darby resisted the temptation to ask him why he'd called if all he was going to do was talk in one- and two-word sentences. He'd have to get around to the purpose of his call eventually.

"Are you busy tonight?"

Darby stifled a gasp. "No, not really." Was he going to ask her out on a date?

"Maybe you should go to Flannigan's Island for a burger," Shane suggested cryptically. Flannigan's Island was a popular restaurant not far from Darby's house. A hangout for the college-age crowd, it was famous for its island motif of indoor palm trees and booths made to look like interiors of little grass huts.

"Why? Are you going to be there?"

"No."

Darby was growing more confused by the minute. "But you think *I* should go there?"

"It would be a good idea."

"I don't understand."

"You don't have to. Just go."

"Shane, what is going on?"

"Have Izzy take you. He's always hungry." And Shane hung up the phone.

It was not Izzy, but Josh whom Darby called next.

"I just had the weirdest conversation of my life with Shane Donahue," Darby said without preamble. "Definitely the weirdest."

"So? Everyone has those kinds of conversations with Shane. He likes to keep everyone on edge."

"He told me to go to Flannigan's Island for a burger tonight."

"He asked you out on a date?"

"No. He told me to have Izzy take me."

"Now that *is* weird!"

"He's got something on his mind. Shane never does anything without a reason. What do you think it is?"

"There's only one way to find out," Josh concluded. "Want to have a burger at Flannigan's tonight?"

————

At seven-fifteen, Josh, Darby, Molly, Kate, and Andrew walked into Flannigan's. Andrew looked around and whistled through his teeth. "I'm glad you called. I've never been here before." He poked at a paper palm tree in the entrance. "Tacky, huh?"

Darby rolled her eyes. She'd thought for a long time about Shane's strange call before deciding to include Andrew and the others in this trip to Flannigan's Island. Perhaps Shane's odd "tip" was nothing, but she had a hunch otherwise. There was *something* that their team was supposed to see here, although Darby had no idea what it might be.

"Andrew, quit being such a snob," Kate chided. "I think it's kind of cute in a childish, inexpensive sort of way."

"Who's the snob?" Andrew retorted. He tipped his nose into the air.

"Break it up, you two. And watch for anything that might help us with our story." Darby was almost getting used to Andrew. She still didn't like his attitude but was beginning to wonder if some of his cocky bluster might not hide a person she actually *could* like. Everybody had secrets, she'd decided long ago. Molly's was the harassment she'd suffered. Who knew what Andrew's might be? Perhaps it was low self-esteem hidden by irritating bravado.

"I can't believe we're doing this," Kate muttered. "Following a 'lead' from Shane!"

"Should we have ignored it?" Darby was beginning to feel a little foolish for organizing this gathering.

"No. I don't think so." Andrew, for once, looked serious. "We all know Shane never does anything without a reason. If *anyone* else had told you to do this, I would have said to ignore it, but Shane . . ."

"Welcome!" A bright, breezy hostess in a colorful sarong greeted them.

She led them to a booth in the center of the building. "It's Hawaiian night here at the Island. Might I recommend the Hawaiian chicken burger and the coconut cream pie? Your waitress will be here in a moment."

"This is some place," Josh commented after the hostess had disappeared. "I've never seen so many artificial pineapples in my life!"

"Or so many college students." Kate glanced around. "I like it here. It's fun."

The large room was noisy. A big-screen television flickered in one corner, and Hawaiian music drifted out of a loudspeaker overhead. "I don't understand what it was that Shane wanted us to see."

"Hi! I'm Mitzi, and I'll be your waitress this evening. Have you decided on your order?"

Mitzi was an attractive blond of about twenty-two. Her hair was bunched into a high-set ponytail just behind her right ear. She wore a lot of makeup and the tightest clothing Darby had ever seen. The shirt was stretched across Mitzi's chest, and the shorts looked as though they'd been painted onto her body. The Flannigan's Island "uniform" looked hardly large enough to fit a child.

Mitzi's eyes narrowed as she caught Andrew's unabashed interest in her costume. "Whatcha staring at, buddy? Haven't you ever seen a waitress before?"

"Aren't you *uncomfortable*?" Kate blurted, then blushed. "I mean, that outfit . . . I'm sorry, I didn't mean to . . . oh, me and my big mouth!"

"I know it's tight," the waitress said, "but it's what the management wants. They give out these uniforms. They say it's good for business." She glanced around the room. "Notice how many men are here tonight? Why do you think we're so busy in here? It's certainly not the food!"

"You mean . . ."

"The food is actually pretty good, but these guys don't care about that. They come to look at the waitresses and their skimpy outfits."

"Don't you mind?" Molly wondered.

"Not if I get big enough tips. I'm a practical person. Besides, I need the money. Why fight it?" Mitzi snapped her gum in her mouth. "Say, are you ready to order or not?"

They ordered, none of them caring any longer what

they ate. The waitress disappeared toward the kitchen, sashaying to cheers and catcalls from the next table.

Molly slapped her hand across her cheek. "Wake me up. Tell me I'm dreaming. Say this isn't happening!"

"That's the sickest thing I've ever seen!" Kate fumed. "She's practically selling peeks at her body for tips! And the management wants it that way!"

"Women aren't *things* to be put on display in order to earn money," Darby fumed.

"I'm so angry and disgusted I could just spit!" Molly said.

None of the boys had said anything until now. In a quiet voice, Andrew commented, "At least now we know why Shane wanted us to come here—and what he wanted us to see."

Molly's head snapped upward, and a knowing look flickered in Kate's eyes. "This is sexual harassment too—just another form."

"We'll have to cover this. It will add another dimension to the story."

Josh gave a low whistle. "Who'd have thought that Shane would steer us onto this. I wouldn't have guessed that he would be this sensitive to an issue like sexual harassment. That boy is thinking all the time! Maybe he's more into the *Live!* program than we thought."

Everyone nodded somberly. They would all look at Shane in a different light from now on.

"Darby, wait up!" Gerilyn McDonald called as she hurried down the hall.

"Hi! How's everything?" Darby greeted her. Gerilyn looked a hundred percent better than the last time Darby had seen her.

"Okay. Better than okay, even." Gerilyn ventured a smile. "And I guess I have you to thank."

"Me?"

"If you hadn't talked to me the other day, and if Ms. Wright hadn't been eavesdropping, I might not have gotten any help."

"Ms. Wright strikes again?"

"More or less. She called my parents and had them come to the school. They talked to Mr. Wentworth about the trouble I'd been having. He was furious that none of this had been reported to him. The school counselor apologized to my parents, the locker rooms have been repainted, and if anyone is caught writing anything in there again, they are to be suspended from school."

"Wow!"

"If only someone could go back and undo the last few weeks. . . ." Gerilyn looked wistful, as if something precious had been taken from her—and it had. Her self-esteem was obviously still in tatters.

"If it makes you feel any better to know this," Darby said, "the guys on the *Live!* staff have been patrolling. If any of them sees or hears anyone trying to make a joke about this, they'll set them straight. We've got some pretty enlightened guys on staff."

"Then say thank you to them as well." Gerilyn smiled and Darby saw how pretty she could be. "I've learned that some people can be very hateful," she admitted, "but I've also learned that some can be pretty terrific as well." Impulsively, she hugged Darby. "And without a doubt, you're in the latter category."

CHAPTER 14

LIVE

FROM BRENTWOOD HIGH

Molly burst into the studio like a whirlwind, hair flying, eyes shining. "What a great day! Don't you just love it?" She dropped her books onto a table and slid into a chair. She leaned back with a satisfied purr.

"Molly, is that you?"

"Of course it's me, Izzy, you big dope. By the way, your socks don't match."

"Sure they do. They're a pair. And I have another pair exactly like them at home." Izzy peered at her unperturbed. "What *happened* to you?"

"Nothing. It's a great day, that's all. I got an *A*-plus on my computer lab, I don't have any homework in accounting, and . . ."

"Since when did you start caring about stuff like that?"

"Since today."

Darby sat down across from Molly. " 'Fess up, Ashton. What happened?"

Molly's infectious laugh drew Gary and Ms. Wright to join the others around the table.

"Oh, I suppose I can tell you—even though it's not public knowledge yet. Mr. Walters has sold the restaurant!"

"That's good?" Kate wondered. "What about your job?"

"I've still got it! My parents discovered that several others had also registered complaints about Mr. Walters with the Equal Employment Opportunities Commission. Now that office is looking into the situation. But what's even better is that Mr. Walters knew he'd gone too far. He sold the restaurant so he could leave town. The new owners are really nice and have promised that I can stay on as part of their staff. Everything is going to be all right!"

"What will happen to Walters?"

"I don't know. My stepdad says that I've worried about this enough. He promised that he'd take care of things." Molly sagged against her chair, the picture of relief. "I'm so glad not to be alone anymore."

"It's what you should have done weeks ago, Molly," Ms. Wright pointed out bluntly.

"I know that now, but at the time I was just so . . ."

"Afraid?"

"Alone?"

"Chicken?"

"All of that and more." There were tears in Molly's eyes. "I didn't know then what wonderful friends and family I had. But I know now, and I want to thank you."

Darby reached to put her arms around Molly just as everyone else reached to do the same. In a moment they were all a wriggling, giggly mass of humanity.

"What's going on in here?" Shane stood in the doorway, looking puzzled and a little put off by the big display of emotion.

Molly struggled out of the center of the mass of people and hurried toward him. When she reached him, she grabbed his face between her palms and gave him a huge, noisy kiss.

Even the ever-cool Shane looked disconcerted. "What was that for?"

"For everything. For understanding more about harassment than I did. For teaching me that guys could be harassed too. For helping us to find out what was going on at Flannigan's Island.

"I feel like a two-ton weight has been lifted off my shoulders. I'm no longer a walking zombie thanks to all of you." Molly beamed at them like a dazzling ray of sunlight.

Shane skulked away, shaken by the overt display of affection.

Gary cleared his throat. "And I'd love to have this celebration continue forever, but we've got deadlines to meet."

"Deadlines!" Molly squealed, her mind fully on her work for the first time in weeks. "We'd better get busy!"

"If we ever have to play kickball in phys. ed. again I'm going to be sick."

"Kickball isn't so bad. It's those stupid relays that get to me. What's the point anyway?" The showers were humming at the end of the physical education hour.

"Good physical health is a gift you give yourself," someone mimicked.

Darby and Molly exchanged a grin. The complaints were the same every day. No one particularly liked phys. ed., but no one had figured out how to completely avoid it either.

"Hurry up in there!" Julie yelled. "I want to take a shower before the boys turn on their side. They take all the hot water."

Darby, who'd been first through the showers, adjusted her collar and picked up her book bag. She and Molly found Sarah outside the locker room on the sidelines of the gymnasium.

"What are you doing?"

"Watching the guys cool down. Coach Henderson must have gotten up on the wrong side of the bed today. He's really crabby."

Darby nodded as she heard the coach begin to bluster.

"Come on, you guys!" he yelled. "You're running like a bunch of girls!"

"Is that the worst thing he could think to call them? 'Girls'?" Helen Jensen commented as she and her friend passed Darby and Sarah.

"They'd better get used to it," the other girl said. "That's how he always talks. Lots of coaches do." The two girls walked on.

Molly began to fume. "Oh! That makes me so mad! That's sexual harassment too! Running down one gender at the expense of another is a rotten thing to do. Doesn't Coach Henderson know any better? What a derogatory, negative, unenlightened comment!"

Sarah attempted to calm Molly with a joke. "You've been hanging around Izzy too much. You're using all those big words he likes."

Molly smiled, but her heart was not in it. "Oh, Sarah, can't *anyone* see that it doesn't do any good to run someone down because he or she is male or female? That's destructive, not helpful.

"If Coach were referring to race, no one here would let him get by with it, but since it's *women* he's running down . . ." Molly trembled with frustration. "Who gave him the right to talk about women that way?"

" 'So God created humankind in his image . . . male and female he created them,' " Sarah said softly.

Molly stared down at Sarah in her wheelchair. "What did you say?"

"I was just quoting a verse from the Creation story in Genesis," Sarah explained. "*No one* has the 'right' to belittle or make fun of one sex over the other. When God created men and women, He made them both in His image—one is not more 'like' God than the other. At least that's the way God planned it."

"Good plan. I *knew* I was right about this. I think I'm going to have a little talk with Coach Henderson. They're almost done with class. He's a reasonable man. I'll just explain to him how offensive that 'running like girls' comment is. And maybe if I tell him it's in the Bible . . ."

Darby and Sarah exchanged a startled glance as Molly trotted off across the floor.

"Can I believe what I'm seeing?" Darby gasped. "She's actually going to do it!"

"It will be fine. Mr. Henderson is a really nice man. He probably didn't think about what he said."

"Well, he will from now on."

Molly cornered him at the far end of the gym as the boys' class ran toward the showers. She was gesturing, emphasizing the points she was making with her hands. Mr. Henderson was nodding solemnly.

"I can't believe the change in her," Darby commented. "She's like a new person. A happy person. A *stronger* person."

"I'm glad," Sarah responded. "She deserved better than the treatment she was getting at work."

"We've all learned a big lesson," Darby concluded. "And, from the looks of things," Darby gazed to where Molly and Mr. Henderson were talking, "she's not going to let anyone forget it!"

CHAPTER **15**

LIVE

FROM BRENTWOOD HIGH

The studio hummed with suppressed excitement. Molly and Josh were about to interview an "expert" on sexual harassment. With Ms. Wright's help, Kate had located a counselor whose specialty was such issues. It would be the crowning touch on an already impressive piece.

Even Mr. Wentworth, the superintendent of the Brentwood school district, had heard about the documentary and asked for a tape of the final product to preview at an upcoming teachers' meeting.

"And now, ladies and gentlemen, we will hear from a prominent Brentwood-area therapist who specializes in treating victims of sexual harassment, Miss Tatania Nyland." Molly looked up from her seat at the news desk. "Does that sound all right? Too pompous? I want to get it right."

"It's fine. You've written four intros already, and every one of them was good." Jake leaned out from behind the camera he was manning. "Relax and enjoy."

"Easy for you to say. No one has to see your face."

"And we can all be grateful for that." Izzy trotted by, wearing patched jeans, a flannel shirt, and a fedora hat.

"What are you doing here, Izz?"

"I came to listen to the interview. Say, has anyone measured the reflected light on Molly?" He pulled a light meter out of his pocket and held it next to her face. "Hmmmm. Looks okay. Good contrast. Just checking."

"Izzy, what did you do before you signed up for this program and got all these gizmos to play with?" Molly asked. Izzy had taken to the technical end of television like a fish to water. His favorite discussions included everything from quad-splits—when the TV screen is split to show four different images—to tilted horizon lines.

"Played with my toes and ate jelly beans, mostly."

"I suspected as much." Molly hadn't expected a rational answer from Izzy.

"Your guest is here." Andrew poked his head into the studio. "I've already briefed her. Are you ready?"

"Ready as I'll ever be." Molly smoothed her hand across the front of her sweater. It was already too warm under the spotlights. "Where's Josh? Let's go!"

———

"As an expert in the area of sexual harassment, could you offer any solutions to the problems which face us?"

Josh and Molly had been grilling their guest for nearly half an hour. Molly's makeup had begun to melt in the warm spotlights, and a sheen of sweat glistened on Josh's forehead. Still, they kept asking questions.

"That's the most difficult question you've asked so far. Solutions to this problem are complex and as varied as each and every differing situation. Still, there are a few ideas about which we can generalize." Miss Nyland still looked surprisingly composed—accustomed, no doubt, to curiosity about her area of specialty.

"We must begin to teach our children early that it is important to get along together. They have to learn that harassment and violence toward those of the opposite sex are wrong. We need to teach respect and cooperation among our youngest students. They need to be aware of the violence and incorrect sexual messages they are seeing on television."

"Can you expand on the kind of sexual harassment that goes on in grade school?" Josh asked.

"There are some very basic misconceptions that need to be corrected. Some children believe there are certain jobs only boys can do. They consider other jobs for 'girls only.' In reality, there are very few tasks that both men and women can't accomplish equally well.

"What's more, we must make our children aware of inaccurate messages in the media. We should teach our children what sexual harassment is—unwelcome touches, suggestive comments, even dirty jokes or photos that are forced upon you."

Miss Nyland grew more animated as she warmed to the subject. "I would encourage businesses and communities to get involved as well. Every business should have its own 'harassment policy,' which sets out guidelines for proper behavior and procedures to follow when that behavior is breached."

"That sounds like a very ambitious plan."

"It isn't easy. Harassment is subtly ingrained into our attitudes and perceptions. That's why I encourage schools to work hard *now* to teach their children to respect one another. It will create fewer problems later on in life—for all of us."

"Is there *anything* we can do right now?" Molly wondered.

"Be assertive. Dress and act professionally at all times. The confidence that gives you will not only make you feel better, but it will also send a message to your co-workers that you are a true professional, not willing to tolerate less from them.

"Develop an aura of strength and determination. Harassers look for victims. If you don't act like a victim, they may pass you by for someone who appears more vulnerable.

"Everyone should be able to have a safe, hassle-free workplace."

As Molly nodded emphatically to Miss Nyland's final statement, Josh wrapped up by saying, "And that concludes our report. For written information and a bibliography of the materials used on this program, please write to us, in care of *Live! From Brentwood High,* Post Office box . . ."

"It's a wrap! Good job, Molly. Josh."

"Thanks for coming, Miss Nyland." Molly's voice lowered so that only Darby and Josh, who were both nearby, could hear her. "Do you have a business card? Just in case I need to talk to you some more."

Josh and Darby exchanged a triumphant look. Molly was taking charge of her life once again.

"Good job. Good job. Good job." Gary was moving through the studio, slapping palms with everyone in the room, just as the school athletes did after a big game.

"Congratulations on a job well done!" Ms. Wright crowed.

"Don't get too happy," Shane commented from where he sat at the back of the studio. "It still needs editing."

"And watching!" Sarah added brightly. "I can hardly wait."

The lunchroom was unnaturally quiet as the televisions mounted from the ceiling flickered to life.

"Are you nervous?" Jake asked Darby and Josh as they joined him at a table.

"Yes. This is the real test. It's easy to impress adults, but kids, on the other hand . . ." The televisions flickered, and the *Live! From Brentwood High* logo flashed onto the screen. Now the real test began.

Darby held her breath until the first rumbles of approval filled the room. Students filed by on their way back to class; several gave a thumbs-up sign.

"Awright!"

"Josh, you looked great. You should be on the six o'clock news."

Darby turned to Josh, who promptly threw his arms around her in a big hug. "We did it!"

"It went over all right too, didn't it?"

"All right? It was terrific." Jake grinned with admiration and pride for his friends. "The interviews were dynamic, powerful, hard-hitting . . . and even the technical stuff looked good." He playfully polished his fingernails on an imaginary lapel. "Thanks to your terrific crew."

"It *was* good, wasn't it?" Darby glanced around the room. "Where's Molly? I have to see what she thinks."

"Would Darby Ellison, Molly Ashton, Andrew Tremaine, Joshua Willis, and Kate Akima please come to the office immediately. Those students again are Darby Ellison . . ."

"Now what?" Josh stared at Darby in alarm at the sound of their names coming across the public address system. "I suppose Mr. Wentworth saw it and didn't like it."

"Don't panic. Maybe he loved it and wants to congratulate us," Darby suggested.

Josh looked doubtful. "Have you *ever* heard of someone being called to Wentworth's office for *good* news?"

"Oh." Darby's smile faded. "I guess not."

The intercom flicked to life again. "Would those students come *immediately* to the office . . ."

————

Ms. Wright and the others were already in the office when Darby and Josh arrived. She was smiling, but the others looked both puzzled and concerned.

"Here they are, Ms. Wright. Will you *please* tell us now what's going on?"

"Are we in trouble?"

"Trouble? Whatever makes you think that?"

"We got called here . . ."

" . . . and that always means trouble!"

"Of course you aren't in trouble! The story was wonderful. I had you paged to come here so I could tell you some *good* news! WWBV just called. They received the previews and tape I sent over this morning. Rather than just send the clip for our ninety second feature, I sent them the entire program—and *they loved it!*

"They're already working on a show on the same subject and want to incorporate your work into their story!"

"*Our* work?"

"Into *their* story?"

"As in 'prime time'?"

"Exactly!" Ms. Wright was so excited her eyes glittered. "Do you realize what this means? They see your piece as professional enough to use in their broadcast!"

"And just think how good this will look on our credentials!" Darby exclaimed, already thinking of the future.

Kate gave a high-pitched squeal and bounced up and down. Even Andrew looked pleased, even though he was not about to go through any physical antics to show it.

It was Josh and Molly, however, who seemed most affected by Ms. Wright's announcement. They stood off to the side, arms around each other. Molly was crying.

"Molly, are you okay?" Kate ventured.

"I never believed that people could cry when they are happy, but it's true." Molly sniffed and blew her nose loudly. "I can't even begin to tell you what I feel like inside. Happy. Relieved. Strong."

"I understand," Josh said softly. "This is proof—real proof—that kids can make a difference. The TV station wants *our* work! Our story is *important*. It could even change lives." He looked awestruck. "I never realized until now how *powerful* television could be."

"That's it." Molly nodded. "Maybe there's someone out there like me who is trapped and scared and who will see this show and realize that she can get help, that she can put a stop to the harassment."

Molly dropped into a chair and stared pensively toward the glass window where she could see students moving through the hallway to their classes. "I didn't think there was a way out, but I was wrong.

"No one will ever take advantage of me in that way again. And if I can do anything to help others, I will. Thank you—all of you—for helping me to learn that."

Mr. Wentworth, who'd been listening from the doorway, cleared his throat. "Ms. Wright," he began, "about this program. I think we *can* discuss your request to expand your project and make it a weekly televison magazine show. I've inquired about airing it on the community access channel as well as here at the school. It appears *Live! From Brentwood High* is here to stay...."

When they gathered again at the studio after school, everyone was giddy over the success of the show. Even Shane looked mildly pleased by the events that had transpired throughout the day.

Andrew had forgotten that it was he who had insisted he didn't believe sexual harassment existed. He was busy taking as much credit as possible for the show's triumph.

"Can you believe him?" Molly grumbled. "You'd think the show had been his idea!"

"But we all know whose idea it really was," Sarah reminded her. "You were very brave, Molly. You inspired a wonderful thing."

"Don't give me too much credit. If I could have taken back that suggestion in the past week, I would have done it in a heartbeat. I'm just glad it worked out."

Darby joined the two girls. "You'd think we'd launched a moon rocket instead of a television show. Josh and Jake are pounding each other on the back till they sound like a pair of war drums."

"Where's Izzy?" Sarah wondered. "He always likes a celebration. He should be here . . ."

Before Sarah could finish speaking, Izzy swaggered into the room, thumbs hooked on the pockets of his jeans. He wore one of his many flannel shirts open at the neck. The face of a dragon blowing puffs of smoke through its nose peeked out from beneath the shirt.

The room grew perfectly silent.

Julie was the first to speak. "Izzy, you *didn't*! Did you?"

"Not a tattoo—not after all we said!"

"Oh, Izzy, how could you?" Dismay tinged Sarah's words.

Izzy might have kept up the charade if it hadn't been for Sarah's horrified expression. As it was, a smile split his face from ear to ear, and he pulled open his shirt, buttons popping. "No, Sarah, I didn't. This is a transfer too." The dragon wound across Izzy's ample belly, and its tail coiled up toward his armpit.

"That is the ugliest thing I've ever seen!" Andrew exclaimed.

"My dragon?"

"No, your stomach. Cover it up before we all get sick. Don't you ever do sit-ups?"

"A hundred crunches a day. I'm in great physical shape, I'll have you know."

"Isador..." Ms. Wright's warning tone stopped Izzy's lunge toward Andrew.

Izzy turned around and grinned. "Actually, this was enough for me—and I got an even better reaction around here than I'd planned! I think I'll go into the teachers' lounge next..."

"What made you decide not to get the real thing?" Gary wondered. "All our scare tactics?"

"Nah. My little sisters told me that they think tattoos are 'yukky.' I had to agree with them. Besides, when I really thought about it, there's no way I'd let anyone touch me with a needle." A flush of embarrassment crept across his features. "If I threw up thinking about a baby being born, I don't know what might happen if I tried to get a tattoo."

"Have you heard the news?" Darby asked.

Izzy shook his head, and the details of the successful reception of their story came pouring out. Izzy beamed with pride.

"That's terrific! What are we sitting around here for?" He dug into his pockets and pulled out a handful of two-for-the-price-of-one coupons. "Pizza's on me!" He gave a little jig with his hips, and the dragon on his chest danced. "Let's party!"

Molly and Darby were the last two out of the studio. Gary and Ms. Wright had offered to drive to the restaurant. Molly looked back as Darby reached to flip out the light. The studio looked large and silent. The cameras hovered along one wall like high-tech, prehistoric monsters. The spotlights, now dark, were like big eyes staring down from the ceiling.

"It's pretty terrific isn't it—all that's happened here already? I never knew how powerful information and education could be," Molly murmured. "I'll never take it for granted again."

Silently Darby nodded. Arm in arm they walked to the cars to meet their friends.

A student is knifed in the halls of Brentwood High. Everyone is shocked, and all are determined to understand how violence could strike so swiftly and so near to home. Is Brentwood High no longer safe? The staff of *Live! From Brentwood High* is determined to find out.

Read Book #3 in the *Live! From Brentwood High* series, *Double Danger*.

A Note From Judy

I'm glad you're reading *Live! From Brentwood High*. I hope I've given you something to think about as well as a story to entertain you. If you feel you have any of the problems that Darby and her friends experience, I encourage you to talk with your parents, a pastor, or a trusted adult friend. There are many people who care about you!

I love to hear from my readers, so if you'd like to receive my newsletter and a bookmark, please send a self-addressed, stamped envelope to:

Judy Baer
Bethany House Publishers
11300 Hampshire Avenue South
Minneapolis, MN 55438